Betrayal of a Thug 2

Lock Down Publications and Ca$h
Presents
Betrayal of a Thug 2
A Novel by *Fre$h*

Betrayal of a Thug 2

Lock Down Publications
Po Box 944
Stockbridge, Ga 30281

Visit our website @
www.lockdownpublications.com

Copyright 2022 by Fre$h
Betrayal of a Thug 2

Lock Down Publications
Like our page on Facebook: Lock Down Publications @
www.facebook.com/lockdownpublications.ldp
Book interior design by: **Shawn Walker**
Edited by: **Kiera Northington**

Stay Connected with Us!

Text **LOCKDOWN** to 22828 to stay up-to-date with new releases, sneak peaks, contests and more…
Thank you.

Submission Guideline.

Submit the first three chapters of your completed manuscript to ldpsubmissions@gmail.com, subject line: Your book's title. The manuscript must be in a .doc file and sent as an attachment. Document should be in Times New Roman, double spaced and in size 12 font. Also, provide your synopsis and full contact information. If sending multiple submissions, they must each be in a separate email.

Have a story but no way to send it electronically? You can still submit to LDP/Ca$h Presents. Send in the first three chapters, written or typed, of your completed manuscript to:

LDP: Submissions Dept
Po Box 944
Stockbridge, Ga 30281

DO NOT send original manuscript. Must be a duplicate.

Provide your synopsis and a cover letter containing your full contact information.

Thanks for considering LDP and Ca$h Presents.

Acknowledgements

I would, first and foremost, like to thank God and give him all the praise he deserves. I thank him for sustaining me in these unfortunate circumstances, and blessing me with this ability and talent, which enables me to write. Writing, in this environment with its constraints and lack of freedom, helps me to escape these walls surrounding me, saving my life both mentally and spiritually.

I looked up the word acknowledgement. It is defined as to admit as to admit as true, to express thanks for, and to recognize as valid. For me the truth is, my family, who I thought was my family, forgot about me at a very devastating and trying time in my life. My grandmother, Margaret Moseley, once told us all, "Never turn your back on family." Looking back, it seems funny to me now because looking at this concrete jungle, I realize I must have been dreaming. I was the only one who heard her sage words of advice.

Rest in peace to my mother, best friend, advocate, and champion through thick and thin, Shirley Ann Dunn. Thank you for always watching over me. Rest in peace to Shelley T. Lamb.

To those who forgot me, THANK YOU! It is because of you that I have been able to find my true strength.

To my oldest son, Malik Barnes, no matter what, thank you for the cartoons, *Chowder*, *Robot Chicken*, and *Adult Swim*.

Last, but never ever least, Alma and Stacie Strickland. Thank you for believing in me and my writing. Without you, Stacie, staying up all night typing my words and giving them life on the page, how could I accomplish this dream and make it a reality? I love you, and I am your biggest fan. When all of the smoke cleared, you had my back. Now we going to get this paper! Big Facts!

To my readers, I salute you for your interest in my vivid imagination. In the words of Jay-Z, my dude, "Put me anywhere on God's green Earth, and I will triple my worth." To Little Dave and William, forever my homies.

Sincerely,
FRE$H

Fre$h

Chapter 1

Weird as it was to have two strangers in her home, which now was our home, Shavonda stayed busy in the kitchen. She made coffee, and then came up to me.

"This is about the situation that took Anthony's life," she said, meaning Laylow.

"They are like family. Han Che was like an uncle to me. If someone killed him, I have to hear Wang and Fujj out. They saved my life," I said, taking the coffee cup from her pretty purple manicured fingers.

"Well, I will just let you all talk. Mr. Wang and Mr. Fujj, is it? Next time, please use the front door," she said to them. Wang and Fujj nodded. She kissed my cheek then walked to the kitchen.

Wang put his coffee down and got right to it. "We have reason to believe Han somehow survived that night from the harbor of that warehouse!" Wang said, looking like he was going to break the chair he sat in. He was five-seven, but weighed three hundred pounds easy, all of it muscle. Fujj, about five-nine, wasn't far behind in build. He looked even more intimidating with the dragon tattoo on his bald head. I was not hearing Wang correctly.

"You telling me after all this time, you think Han is still alive? Bullshit! I was informed that area was combed the same night by Mr. Diplo's men. It was fucking freezing that night. Shit, the warehouse was on the outskirts of Chesapeake, what makes you think this?" I said, now sitting down.

"Because Yayo Sun, we have eyes and ears. Plus, the Triad has been active more lately," Wang said and Fujj grunted his agreement.

"The Triad is more active. What does that mean?" I said, rolling a blunt, trying to figure out how these two big ass dudes tiptoed in my kitchen. *I'm glad they are on my side.*

"I have a friend inside who says a new member was recruited six months ago. The knowledge they have of, not all but some of, our operations is not good. But no one knows the info this new recruit has been spilling, but four men on this side of the sun. That's me, Fujj, Han Che, and of course Han," Wang said, trying to convince me.

"If that's true, then Han can be recognized. Right? We just find him, send him with Nikoli, and it's done," I said, smoking the Purple Haze. It was Shavonda's favorite.

"Yayo Sun, it's not that simple. We believe if this is Han, he has changed his appearance." Wang nodded to Fujj. Fujj dug in his coat pocket and pulled out pictures. He put them on the table. There were about five or six of them. I looked them over. The dude I was looking down at damn near looked like the late great Bruce Lee.

"Yo... Wang, this cat looks like Bruce Lee, man. So, you really think this is Han?" I said, trying to pass the blunt to them. They both declined my offer. Maybe it was a Chinese thing, but I remembered Han smoked a lot of weed.

"I don't *think* anything, Yayo Sun. I know it's Han," Wang said, sipping the coffee now. Fujj grunted his agreement with Wang. "Before Han Che's death, he felt a little uneasy. Months ago, he had a map, and we drove out to that warehouse early in the morning. When I asked why we were out there, he told me he was thinking about buying some of the land. Han Che, of course, was complicated like that. I've been around Han Che for fifteen years, Yayo Sun. I have not ever heard knowledge of a body turning up when we took that ride," Wang said.

"Shit, maybe the gators got him, and I didn't shoot him in the leg," I said, thumping ashes in my Tommy Hilfiger ashtray. "But I can't lie, Wang," I said, shaking my head.

"You weren't sure he was dead, either way," Wang said.

"It bothered me, but Han Che dead, I don't believe in coincidence." I looked at the picture. There was something about it I noticed as I shuffled through them.

It's the nose, isn't it?" Wang said.

"Yeah, the nose on this guy is beyond wrong," I said, looking at the pictures. I thought back to some guy that owed Han, and they were fighting in the parking lot. We were teenagers then. I came over, and we both ended up kicking the guy's ass together. Anyway, I swung at the guy, and he ducked my jab. I broke Han's nose. After we finished kicking the shit out of this dude, we were riding back in his Jetta. He was cursing me out for getting in the fight, but we were cool then. We laughed it off over a joint later that night. Yeah, the nose was real familiar. I push the pictures back toward Wang. Fujj pocketed them. "How did Han Che die?" I asked.

"He always loved drinking that Louis XIII cognac. Well, there was a power outage a week ago. We think that is when someone snuck in and poisoned the bottle. It was that morning we found him in his study, glass spilled over, leaned back in his chair. He choked on his own vomit. He was in bad shape, Yayo Sun," Wang said behind his all-black Louis Vuitton shades.

"Okay, so what's the plan then? How are we going to know this guy actually is Han?" I asked.

"Easy. We find someone to get a blood sample. Once we test it, if it's a match, he will no longer breathe," Wang said. Fujj grunted his agreement.

"Alright, but who the hell is going to do that? If it's Han, he will see any of us a mile away," I said, not believing there was a chance Han had actually escaped death, though he had managed to stage his first one. There was one thing I knew. If he was alive, I would kill him. The shit I had gone through was unforgivable.

I know Milk Marie and I were not together, but that was some true scumbag shit. Shavonda was my heart now. I didn't want to lose her, but I had them in my kitchen. Maybe Han was going to kill me. Maybe not. I owed it to Han Che.

"We will figure that part out. I'll get back with you because some important people are on their way from China for the funeral. Once I come to you with what I come up with, we can get to the bottom of this," Wang said, done with his coffee. "You will need to travel."

"Travel? Travel to where exactly?" I asked, taking Wang and then Fujj's coffee cups.

"These pictures you saw was a Triad operation in Atlanta. They stepped on our feet a little, and that's how we got these pictures," Wang said.

"Wang, how do you know so much about the Triad? Why would Han, if it is Han, work with the same people who killed his mom?" I asked, confused. All of this was too much to register at this time of the night.

Wang leaned closer to me, peering through those dark Louis Vuitton shades. "You are smart, Yayo Sun. Han was full of hatred, and he blamed Han Che for Mrs. Charlotte's death. You can't take the throne because he got exposed when Milk Marie told Patron. Then Patron contacted us. Therefore, we tracked you to the warehouse. You cannot be a successor, so you use the opposite side to bring down the empire. You plotted to control but failed," Wang said.

"Then on top of that, let's say, Han did survive that night and it was exposed. The Chinese and the Russians would swarm him," I said, feeling no remorse for a friend who was now a foe.

"All the more reason to believe the scenario that's in front of us. If we are wrong, then we still get rid of this Ken Chew, which is Han's alias. If, in fact, it is Han. If it is or is not, he still dies for the disrespect of stepping on the cartel's toes in Atlanta," Wang said, checking his Rolex. Both were in black Armani suits, no tie, only a red handkerchief in the top pocket. This symbolized a top dog had passed on.

"So, tell me, Wang. How do you know so much about the Triad? I know I'm a young black man, but there is more to me than fried chicken and basketball," I said seriously. "Han Che was like a godfather to me. He always took me and Han for ice cream. Let us stay up all night for sleepovers. This gorgeous redbone asked me to take her to the prom. Before the Maybach, the Lamborghini Aventador gave me a lot of praise at the prom, thanks to Han Che loaning it to me. A two-hundred-thousand-dollar car, and I was pulling up at my high school. I gave a fuck about Han Che, just like they did. I never had a dad, so I am thankful for Han Che's kindness." Wang sensed I wanted answers.

"Yayo Sun, Han Che came from nothing. His mom sold her body. His father was an alcoholic. The cartel took him at fourteen years old. By sixteen, he was a lieutenant. As you may know, he and Han Che had issues because of Charlotte. A few men died because of that feud," Wang said. Then for the first time since I've known Wang, he removed his shades. He had only one eye.

"I was in the Chinese Triad. So was Fujj. Han Che was ruthless and did something that made me join up with him, as did Fujj," Wang said, putting his shades back on.

"Shit, Wang! What happened to your eye?" I said, now understanding why in all these years, he had never taken them off.

"I don't know about these gangs you Americans may have, but we give blood for loyalty. The same blood you shed in battle with your foes. To be able to leave the Triad, other than by death, you have to part with something. Therefore, I gave my eye and Fujj his tongue." Wang stood as he went on. "I would see my way through my decision and Fujj would never speak anything against the Triad. We have been with Han Che ever since," Wang said, walking towards the kitchen door which led outside. The air was fresh and perfumed with a hint of the rain that was to come.

"I will be in touch with all the details, and I am sorry for startling your lady friend," he said, with Fujj clapping me on the shoulders as he walked by. "Get some sleep, Yayo Sun. The days ahead may be long." As he started to walk off, the light pole shined on them, two huge figures in the night.

"Hey, Wang! With Han Che gone, who is the boss?" I asked. Wang turned to me with the flow of the light glinting on him, as Fujj turned as well. Wang lifted his shades once more, and he winked his milky white eye at me, saying, "I am the boss!"

Chapter 2

Can I Live...

Some days had gone by, and it was almost shocking to see the sight at Han Che's funeral. I had never been around so many foreign people in my life. People flew in from Haiti and the Virgin Islands. There were even a few famous people in attendance, like Steven Segal, a longtime friend of Han Che. The guitarist from Nirvana was also there as well as a sea of Chinese men and women. All were in tailored suits and expensive couture dresses bidding a final farewell to, in the eyes of many, a businessman. To those of us who knew better, Han Che, the drug lord. I walked up to Han Che's casket with a lone red rose in my hand. I put it on top of the casket's dark exterior and whispered, "Safe journey, homie."

His casket was custom-made, black onyx. There was red Chinese writing on the top. I left with Shavonda, arm in arm. She looked beautiful. She was wearing an all-black Kate Spade dress with gold trim around the neckline and gold Ferragamo stilettos. She wore bronze lipstick, perfect against her bronzed, sun-kissed skin from a recent trip to the beach. She also held a black Ferragamo purse with a gold chain as the shoulder strap. Me, I had on an all-black Gucci suit with gray, black, green, and red Gucci loafers. All-black Gucci shades covered my eyes, dreads in a ponytail. We stood by and watched a private jet load up his casket for the trip back to China. Once the plane was in the air, Wang walked over to me.

"In three days, come by the mansion. We will talk. Things will work itself out, as Han Che used to say." We hugged. I walked off, seeing Patron. He was in an all-gray Polo pinstripe

15

suit and black Polo dress shoes. I know he liked Polo, but he looked like a lawyer.

"What up, Yay? Damn man, shit real if some nigga whacked Han Che," Patron said, rubbing his waves. "So, you know who did it yet?"

Lisa, Patron's girl, and Shavonda were talking a few feet away from us.

"Man, you wouldn't believe me if I told you," I said to Patron.

"Try me because the warehouse was some crazy shit by itself. So, what up? Who popped Han Che?"

"First of all, no one popped him. He was somehow poisoned. Someone slipped something in his liquor," I said, ready to leave. I hated funerals.

"Okay, so how did he get that way? Come on, Yay. Don't hold out on me," Patron said.

I looked around, then I leaned in his ear. "They think Han is alive, and somehow he did it," I told Patron.

"Yo, that's a swimming motherfucka. Damn warehouse was in the middle of a nowhere. Shit, it was freezing that night. Fool lucky, but how they know?" Patron said.

"I don't know exactly, but Wang and Fujj getting info on it. Sorry bastard might have even got a facelift," I said, irritated.

"What do you think?" Patron asked.

"I think he played dead one time. Let's make sure he dead this time," I said.

Patron gave me a pound on my fist. "And that's a fact bruh. I'll see you at your spot. Let the ladies chat while we talk some things over. I'm ready to bounce," Patron said.

"I'm with you," I said. We took the ladies and left, hoping to make sense of this mess.

***

Once at my house, Lisa and Shavonda were in the kitchen. Patron and I were in the living room, rolling some sour diesel.

"Damn, man, remember when Han had that fine ass Chinese girl he hooked me up with?" Patron said, lighting the blunt.

"Yes," I said grinning, "I remember," trying not to laugh.

"I mean, she was fine! She was giving me crazy head with her shades on." Patron started grinning. "Fuck you laughing at? You and Han were in the kitchen laughing because the bitch was blind. I wondered why she kept feeling for my face."

I busted out laughing. Patron was bringing her out of the room when she bumped into the wall. Shit was too funny!

"Yeah, Han was funny like that. Remember when Han had got a hundred-K loan on the Lamborghini? They repo'd the damn car," I said laughing.

"Fuckin Han found the guy that repo'd it, got his car back, and super glued the guy's lips together," Patron said.

"Yeah, that cost Han Che some bread. Isn't that how you got that Larry dude?" Patron asked, blowing out clouds of smoke.

"Yeah, and speaking of him, he didn't stay at the funeral long. I think he gestured for me to call him. This whole thing got me bugging. I was thinking of marrying Shavonda," I said to Patron, admitting it for the first time.

"Wow, man! I am glad you found someone. It got to be weird though, now you got a son with Milk Marie," Patron said, passing the blunt.

"Shavonda doesn't like it, but she said she knew there was already Milk Marie. I just don't like the fact sometimes. I miss her though I shouldn't," I said, shaking my head.

"No shit, the bitch fucked Han, then had the nigga come back from the dead for that pussy. Shit, you two were tight for a while. I liked you two together until that bullshit with Han," Patron said, pouring himself another shot of Goose.

"Yea that was some grimy shit, but she wasn't my girl and shit like that is why I am like I am. But Shavonda…" I stood up liquor and loud pack got me. "Shavonda got a big ole booty, sexy as hell and throw it back like a stallion," I said, talkin like a reverend.

"Preach, brotha, preach!" Patron said grinning.

"It something, something 'bout that booty."

"Amen to the booty!" Patron said laughing.

Clearing her throat, Shavonda said, "What you two Negroes in here laughing about?" Shavonda and Lisa stood, shaking their heads at us.

"Just talking about both of you beautiful women and pointing out your blessed features," I said.

"Amen, amen!" Patron yelled, grabbing Lisa.

"Lord, girl! They in here trippin. I'm driving, Terrence," Lisa said, hugging Shavonda. Lisa was the only, I mean the only person that called him that.

"Yo, homie, when Wang and Fujj holla at you, then holla at me. You hear me?" Patron said seriously.

"I got you no doubt, fam," I said, walking them out the door. I went in the kitchen and rolled up Purple Haze, which was also Shavonda's favorite color. Once I rolled it, I automatically lit it. I heard Shavonda behind say "Smoking back-to-back, I see." She took the blunt, inhaled once and blew out smoke. She would always start giggling. I felt that made the mood a lot lighter, but Shavonda started to get to know me.

"So, this issue you had is not finished, I assume?" Shavonda said, looking at me with those beautiful green eyes of hers. Redbone and thick in all the right places. I was hoping for more. I really liked her.

"Just some unfinished business. Hopefully, it will be taken care of in the next few months, baby," I said, taking the blunt into the bedroom. I laid on my back and Shavonda crawled on top of me.

"Yo, what up? Why you all in my grill?" I asked, blowing smoke in her face. She slapped my face playfully.

"First of all, I'm your girlfriend and I'm in your grill like a cavity. Whatever you about to do, baby, come back to me," she said, digging in my waist, pulling out my Desert Eagle and laying it on my stomach. "With your gun in your hand, on those two feet." Tears cascaded down her face.

"Baby, I promise you I will come back on both feet, same way I came into your life. Got to make sure things can stay the way they are. I want nothing more than to be with you. I don't want anything else in the way of us. Okay?" I said, wiping the tears from her sun-kissed cheek.

"Okay. I know it's been a year, but I love you, boy. You understand I love being with you, Yay, but the kind of people you know scare me."

"Well, those I really don't know are what bother me most. Once everything is in order, we should be good," I said, putting the blunt out. Shavonda kissed my forehead, got up from the bed, ass bouncing from left to right. She went to the door and locked it, bit her bottom lip and started undressing. I kicked my Gucci loafers off and loosened up my shirt. It had been a long day. The stereo system in the bedroom was playing. Post Malone sang, "I'm saucin, I'm saucin on you. I'm swaggin, I'm swaggin on you."

Only things Shavonda had on were her Prada bra and panties. She walked up to me and licked my neck, then kissed it. I began to caress her huge ass. She whispered in my ear, "Those guys, are they really cartel?"

"Yes. Wang is the boss now. Fujj is the muscle," I said, kissing her neck.

"So, you're like in the mob basically? I'm sorry, but shit is turning me on. Do me a favor?" she said, licking her lips and getting on her knees.

"What's the favor?" I felt her pulling my dick out of my pants. Felt her breathing on it.

"Feed mami this dick," Shavonda said, swallowing me.

Chapter 3

Seek and Ye Shall Find

A few days went by and today, Wang had assured me we could get this Ken Chew's DNA. The year that had flown by was good to me. Two months ago, I had bought a Lamborghini, all-black with a green and red stripe down the middle. The whole interior was Gucci. Once you drive luxury cars and see the looks on people's faces, it's hard not to enjoy the attention.

I was on my way to the mansion that was Han Che's, but what I now assumed Wang had inherited. The mansion was in Emerald Island, which was a whole other world from the hood. Butlers came to the door, and I've seen them have tea ready as soon as they pull up.

Once I pulled up to the mansion, two men were flanked at the long driveway. Fujj was at the door nodding at me. Once I walked in, I felt like I was in a damn auditorium, surrounded by Chinese artifacts. I got on an elevator with Fujj and ascended to the second floor of the mansion. At the door, Fujj grunted at me and opened the door. As I stepped through, Fujj closed it behind me and stood guard on the other side. I was greeted by portraits of Samurai warriors, and a dark brown Persian rug covered the marble floor. I had only been in the mansion a few times.

It is something I assumed, but I always felt Han Che had someone else over him. So being Han couldn't take the throne, I guess somehow Wang was next in line. The fireplace was the size of a small cave. It was cozy in what I'm guessing was, the living room. The room was half the size of a basketball court. Huge, chocolate brown sofas were spaced out just right, a few feet from the fireplace. Wang stood up from a laptop he was looking at on a mahogany table.

"Yang Sun, it's always good to see you, my friend. I wanted to run a proposition by you. I've been doing my homework lately, and getting the DNA is important," Wang said in a gray, tailor-made Armani suit. There was someone else sitting on the far end of one of the couches. Her hair was long, covering one side of her face. Wang was walking me away from her to another sitting area as he talked.

"Ken Chew is supposedly the go-to guy to get things done. He raids shops to pay for protection all over Atlanta. Even has his hands in the malls. When I say Ken Chew stepped on our toes in Atlanta, I'm talking five million," Wang said at the mini bar.

"Five million is a lot of damn toes, Wang," I said, whistling out loud as I watched Wang pour two drinks with a little crushed ice. I took my drink and sipped it. It was Knob Creek Kentucky Bourbon Whiskey.

"I know you don't sip brown, but that's all I got. We threw out a case of the Louis XIII cognac. Everyone calls it the dead man's drink because of what happened to Han Che. Anyway, I got a line on Ken Chew. He liked to drink at Mason Fine Arts Gallery," Wang said, while flipping through a file. "Two Triad bodyguards are with him at all times."

"Mason Fine Arts Gallery… What is that, like a museum or something?" I asked, still wondering who the lady sitting on the far end of the couch was. There was something about her hair, but I didn't know why I cared. Things like that bug you when you feel something familiar.

"No, Yay, it's like a restaurant, cook out, mini party feel. People with a few bucks can hobnob over wine, certain recipes are made on the spot. There is art on the walls by Van Gogh and Picasso," Wang said.

"Sounds like a café for stuck-up people you ask me," I said, finishing my whiskey.

"That's exactly what it is, but it's still tasteful to move in these circles. See we had property that somehow got purchased by Ken Chew. Our brokers, of course, said all transactions were through a woman's name. But ask yourself, why go through all of that to buy property? There is no coincidence this happened. He is inching his sights towards the family. I don't know if it's still the bad blood of Han Che or He, or is it just business? Either way, I don't like it. Getting that property was the red flag that made me dig deeper," Wang said.

"And what exactly did you find? It's still hard to tell if Han is alive," I said.

"That is why we are getting the DNA to be sure it's him, but if it's not him, then Ken Chew is just a threat I'm recognizing. I'll let Han rest, but guess what else is ironic about this issue?" Wang asked.

"What's that, Wang?" I said, rolling a blunt of hydro up with a Garcia Vega.

"Someone in this area is on his Facebook and seems to show interest, but I need for you to think on why it's ironic. I told you I don't believe in coincidence." Wang stood up from the plush couch and said, "Dear lady, please join us so we can address this issue more properly," Wang said.

I heard the high heels first hit the marble floor, and as she got closer, it was the hair that was different. Instead of dark brunette, it was black as night. All-white Chanel dress that hugged every curve, all-white Prada heels with the red bottoms. Her nails and lipstick were pink.

"Milk Marie, what are you doing here? I mean, you look nice," I said, lighting the blunt. I didn't know what to say. "Wang, what's going on?"

"Ken Chew is on Milk Marie's Facebook, which he started by finding Milk Marie on Instagram, but Milk Marie didn't pay it any mind," Wang said, looking at Milk Marie.

"So, when I was waiting to have the baby, Wang contacted me and asked me things about Han." Milk Marie paused for a minute. She stared down at her nails and studied them for a moment. She sat down and said, "I told him I lost you because I was stupid. That whatever I could do I would to make things right. Then Wang asked me if I knew of anyone named Ken Chew. I knew I had heard the name but couldn't remember. Well, when I had Malcolm, I took pictures of us on Instagram. That's when I knew the name," Milk Marie said.

"Wait a minute. So, you were on Chew before Han Che was killed? So, why you weren't on it then? What's the difference now?" I asked, smoking the blunt.

"The info came maybe a day before Han Che got killed. We talked about it, but like you, I wasn't truly realizing. I felt Han Che knew, but after we found him dead. The next day, the property was sold. So, I kept connecting the dots. So here we are. You think I'm crazy, but Han Che has my loyalty. It feels too close to the truth," Wang said.

"Okay, so basically Ken Chew is a thorn in your side. Somehow, he has a little intel on some of your operations. If we do get the DNA and it's not Han, then either way, Ken Chew gets erased," I said, understanding everything now. Getting the DNA is just the curiosity Wang feels Han Che had. After that, I guess Wang would handle it from there. I could just keep it pushin with Shavonda.

"As always, Yayo Sun, you are good with words," Wang said.

"So, when do we flush him out, Wang? I want to be sure this is over. I just want a clean slate," Milk Marie said, glancing at me.

"In time, my dear. In the meantime, you keep playing hard to get with Ken Chew until we get more intel," Wang said, looking at me for approval.

"So basically, Milk Marie is bait for us to get to Ken Chew," I said, puffing the blunt, trying to not to notice how sexy Milk Marie looked. Then I remembered why Han Che never ate apples. I just shook my head, laughing to myself.

"What's so funny, Yayo Sun? Would you like to share?" Wang asked.

"It's just that Han Che was so right about a lot of jewels he dropped on me. I'm thankful for that. Just thinking about something he said," I said, crushing the blunt in a silver ashtray.

"Well, okay then. Ken Chew is smitten by Ms. Johnson here. He frequents the Mason Fine Arts Gallery. As I said, two guys are with him at all times. He has some investment in Tiffany & Co., to what degree, I don't know. Ken Chew is in Phipps Plaza quite a bit daily, Wang said.

"That's the Simon Center. It's like a mall, but designer only. I think Saks Fifth Avenue and Versace, just to name a few are sold there in Atlanta." I shopped there, once I started to stack up some money. See, I learned the flashy stuff like jewelry, cars with custom rims, etc. drew attention. When you get your money up, you want the haters to witness you come up, but we are talking a few bricks and too many baby mamas. No, we were wealthy and though I still had my days, I cut the flash down. I learned to be low key. When I first met Milk Marie, I had a burgundy Cutlass on twenty-four-inch-rims. Now, I drive a Lamborghini and that's a big difference.

"Right and this is why I want to be sure of my suspicion. Please have your affairs in order. Once I call upon you, I'll need you to be ready to leave," Wang said.

Then the whiskey hit me. I felt a good buzz from the drink. Then I remembered something. "Han Che owned a whiskey company in Atlanta and a jewelry store in Atlanta, I think," I said.

"Right, and we have a lot of business in Atlanta. That property should not have been sold, even though it made us a good profit. In three years, that number would have tripled with shopping malls, liquor store. Hell, maybe even a Walmart," Wang said.

I stood up. I had on an all-gray Gucci linen suit, Gucci shoes, and Gucci frames. I tried my best never to mix designers. For instance, I would never rock Jordans with a Reebok shirt on. If Han Che had on Versace, then trust me, his socks were also Versace. Out of all the jewelry I had, I only rocked my necklace with my mom's picture, and the twenty-four-karat gold on all my teeth.

"Well, Wang," I said, shaking his hand, "I'll be ready once you call, and I'll be getting my affairs in order." I glanced at Milk Marie, looking like Megan Fox from the movie *Transformers.* The pink lipstick looked so moist. I nodded to her and began to walk out the room. I couldn't believe Wang thought Han was alive. I wasn't convinced. I felt Wang just wanted Ken Chew out of the way. Man, five million was a lot of money to be in the way of. Shit, I knew people from my hood who would kill you for their first month's rent. Taking me out my thoughts, Wang cleared his throat loudly.

"Excuse me, Yay. I have some matters to attend to. I had Milk Marie picked up. Please be a gentleman and assist her home." He then lit a cigar and walked out the room. The sweet smell of the smoke and the silence was too much.

"I can get a ride if it's an issue," Milk Marie said, smacking her lips, all polite manner gone with ghetto attitude. "I know I'm just the baby momma."

"Look, it's cool, I'll give you a ride. Because Wang knows I will for one, and for two, no one is permitted out here. Whoever foolish enough to drive out here would be killed on sight and their car plus the body would vanish," I said.

"Damn, it's like that around here?" Milk Marie asked shocked.

"Han Che is dead. Someone got on these grounds and poisoned his liquor. Damn right, it's like that, but I meant what I said." I looked her up and down. "You do look nice."

Once in the car, the radio was playing Two Chainz. "When I die, bury me inside the Gucci store. When I die, bury me in the Louie store. All I want for my birthday is a big booty girl..."

Milk Marie turned the radio down and turned in her seat to look at me. "Do you really think Han is alive?" she asked.

"Honestly, I was there, and so were you. I shot him in the foot. It was freezing that night. I don't think it's likely. It's been a year. Wang just wants Ken Chew out of the way," I said.

"Yay, I know we aren't as close as we used to be," she said.

"Don't start, Milk. That's the past. I just want to kill Wang's curiosity and get on with my life," I said.

"I guess your life with Shavonda is the life you talking about?" She took a deep breath. "She seems nice though."

"So does your manager at Peabody's. I know you have other kids. Just don't have no nigga all around my son, and we good," I said, pushing the foreign.

"Excuse me, *our* kid and I'm grown, last time I checked. But I am glad we are at least speaking. So, if the baby wasn't yours?" she said.

I looked at her fingers, squeezing the steering wheel. Trying to keep my composure because Milk Marie knew how to get under my skin.

"Then I wouldn't be having this conversation because you would be a ghost," I said, putting my eyes back on the road.

"Damn it, Yay, you act like you're perfect. Fine then, but I almost died because of all this. Last time I checked, so did you. I'm telling you this Ken Chew," she spoke through teary eyes. "He is creepy like Han was. If it's true, I'll kill him myself. Maybe one day you'll forgive me." Then she wiped her eyes, and they changed from sorrow to lust. This was the Milk Marie I knew. "Damn, I miss fucking you though."

My cell phone was ringing. I was grateful for the interruption because the smell of Chanel N° 5 on Milk Marie was killing me.

"Yo, what's up?" I answered.

"Yay, I need you to come to my house pronto, homie," Patron said on the other end.

"What's up, man? Everything good? You sound like you opened your safe and realized no money was in it," I said, being funny.

"Hey, Patron," Milk Marie yelled.

"Yo, is that Milk Marie?" Patron asked.

I shook my head because I knew where this was going. "Yes, man. Yes, it's Milk Marie. I'm dropping her off at her apartment."

"You sly dog. I knew you two were going to end up fucking around." Patron laughed.

I was getting agitated because I knew Wang set me up.

"Man, I'm just giving her a ride. Wang got me on a damn wild goose chase. I think I'm going to Atlanta in a few days," I said, glancing at Milk Marie nodding her head to the Two Chainz song. She had kicked her shoes off and even her toes were pink. I felt myself smiling. When you haven't seen some-one in a while, you notice so many things. For a white girl, she was still fly, but she was the mother of my son and nothing more.

"Atlanta? Shit, I'm going! All those big booty chicks out there. Look, come to the house. I got an issue," Patron said with a touch of desperation in his voice.

"I'm on my way. Broke niggas make noise," I said in the phone.

"Rich niggas make moves," Patron said, hanging up.

Luckily, Milk Marie called a friend of hers, and I didn't have to drive her all the way home. She said her mom had little Malcolm, and they were getting along. The girl in the Jeep looked at me, and I felt I had seen her somewhere.

"Well, my little trollop, are you coming along or not? I have engagements to keep, yeah!" the girl with the English accent said to Milk Marie as I lifted up the door to let her out of my Lamborghini.

"Don't pay her no mind. That's just Vicky. She's from England. She comes in the Peabody a lot. Anyway, hope to see you later." Milk Marie kissed me on the check and then whispered in my ear, "She can't suck you or fuck you like me. Remember that."

I kissed her back on the cheek, while staring into Vicky's eyes and I whispered into her ear, "Remember this. Disloyalty is not rewarded but thank you for Malcolm."

Milk Marie gave me a sad look, then got in the Jeep with Vicky. As they drove off, Vicky kept staring at me. I could have sworn I heard her say, "Oh, so that's the baby daddy, my love?" but I brushed it off.

I went zero to sixty in my Lamborghini to Harvest Heights, where Patron lived. I tried to tell Patron to put his sporting goods store on the beach with Shavonda's All Goods Here store, but he kept his store location in Elizabeth City by the Walmart area. I didn't like driving my car in the city. Jealous cops would take forever to let me go after they pulled me over. In Virginia Beach, everyone had an expensive car. So, blending in wasn't an issue. Plus, I hate city cops. Once I pulled up, Patron immediately came out and got in the car and told me to drive to his store.

When I pulled up to the store, he hopped out, and rushed me to walk around back. It was still fairly early. I think a little after lunch.

Once in the store, he set the alarm code. He had a built-in basement, where we would hide our supply at times, or throw parties when we had the time. No one knew of the basement but me and Patron.

Patron cut on all the lights when we got down there. The smell was the first thing to hit me. "Yo, Patron, what the fuck you got going on?"

Chained to the wall was some guy, beaten bloody with a gag in his mouth. I mean, we had money, so what the hell was this about?

"I know what it looks like, but this piece of shit," Patron said while kicking him, "was my groundskeeper. This fool cut my front and back lawn, not to mention, the front lawn of the store."

"Okay, but you don't kidnap your fucking gardener, homie. Nigga looks damn near dead. How long he been down here?" I asked Patron.

"Three days. My dilemma is his wife knows where I live. Came asking about him earlier, said my house was the one he was supposed to do, then come home after." Patron got in the guy's face. "But you never made it home, did you? Huh? You perverted piece of shit." Then, Patron spit on him.

"Whoa, Whoa! For one, the fuck you bring me in this for? And two, what did he do?" I asked, looking at the guy, shaking my head. His nose was broken, and his left eye was swollen closed. It was obvious he had shit and pissed on himself. Damn, three days like that.

"Okay, we got three bathrooms and one is on the second floor. Lisa was taking a shower, which at this time, this piece of shit is on a ladder. Bruh, instead of trimming the vines on the side of the house, this fool is masturbating looking at my fucking girlfriend." Patron viciously kicking him.

"Whoa! Whoa! Chill, man. Let's figure this out, okay?" I said, pushing Patron back.

"Don't fucking judge me, Yay. You didn't see the fucking video. He lucky he already not dead." Patron had saliva flying out of his mouth.

Today was turning into one of those days already. I just wanted to kick back with Shavonda. Had to fix this shit. I held Patron back and walked up to the dude. I took the gag out of his mouth. He was handcuffed to the wall. So were his feet. We had some stripper chicks over a month ago. Patron was a freak. He got a guy to install the cuffs in the wall. Rich chicks were the freakiest.

He started coughing and spitting up saliva, gasping for air. The guy was fucked up, but he would live.

"What's your name, man?" I asked, wiping my hands on a cloth on the desk in the room.

"James. James Richards," he said, coughing. "Look, man, p-please don't kill me. I d-didn't mean to do it." He stuttered, pleading for his life.

"Shut the fuck up, pussy. You were on a ladder beating your dick, looking at my girl. Talking about you didn't mean it," Patron said cocking his nine-millimeter. "Move, Yay. They can't hear shit down here."

"Oh, please, please..." the guy begged.

"Yo... chill, man! Give me that shit." I took the gun from Patron. I then smacked the guy upside the head with it. "And you, you shut the fuck up. Lisa is family and you lucky you alive. I'm assuming you got his wallet?" I said to Patron.

"Yeah, I got it." Patron started reading, "James Richards, 110 Salem Drive, Edenton, NC. This fool got a picture of his fat ass wife and two daughters. You got two girls. Would you want someone doing that shit to them?" Patron yelled.

I kneeled down, looked this James guy in the eyes. "You want to live, man?" He nodded his head. "Do you own your lawn care business?" He nodded yes. I took a deep breath and stood up.

"Okay, for a year, all the monthly gross comes to us. After that, the beginning of that first year, half the taxes you acquire goes to us. Then, you'll be free from us. You say you got video footage, right, Patron?" I questioned.

"Yes, I got cameras all around my house. This fool must didn't see them," Patron said with murder in his eyes.

"Okay then, if you miss one damn payment, I will put the video on *YouTube*, *Instagram*, and you and your business will be done. I'm sure your wife and two daughters would be ashamed after the video. We clear on this?" I said to James. He just nodded to us.

I got his size from him and got him a cheap jumpsuit, shoes, socks, and boxers from Walmart. After we got him cleaned up, we took him to his lawn care truck parked behind Dairy Queen. Patron had kidnapped the nigga and parked his work truck. None of us ever had normal lives. I mean, how many friends do you have that when you come to chill with them, they got a nigga hostage? I gave the guy numbers to an offshore account. I was trying to keep the guy alive.

We went back to Patron's store, and I helped him clean the basement. "Yo what has gotten into you?" I asked him.

"Don't do that, Yay. You probably killed more niggas than me," Patron said.

"I wouldn't have brought him to the basement of my business though. Plus, you said his wife was looking for him," I said.

"I know, I know, but hey, it could have been worse." Patron was putting all the cleaning supplies in a bag to be thrown out.

"How could it have been worse?" I asked, rolling up some sour diesel.

"I was going to cut his dick off and mail it to his damn wife," Patron informed me, grinning.

"Damn, so this means you serious about Lisa, huh?" I said, pulling the blunt after I lit it.

"Yeah, I guess so. Damn, I had to kidnap a nigga to know I was in love." We both started laughing as Patron opened the store for business.

Fre$h

Chapter 4

Excuse Me Miss...

I was up about 3:00 am from having another bad dream. Only this time, I was holding Han Che as the rain poured. I kept replaying the night Han got shot. Now Han Che was dead, and Wang thought Ken Chew was Han's ghost. I needed to get away, and even though I still did business with Wang, I had stepped it up and got a connection out of Spain. He was in Virginia Beach with a young girl and wife back in Spain. His name was Jefe Martinez. He preferred to be called El Jefe, the boss.

San Sebastian, Spain, has the three best restaurants in the world, and El Jefe owned all three. I had only known him for five months, but he reminded me of Han Che. I'd only been twice, and I decided to take another trip. Not only was I getting my affairs in order, but this would be my biggest shipment. See, El Jefe got it delivered to you. How he did it, I don't know, but it was extremely convenient.

El Jefe would say, "I got guys in the past, I would allow them to pick up the keys themselves, you know. But you can say lies as if you got caught, or had to get rid of the work." He paused. "Well, it upsets me because this is my city. As in your country the authorities harass you, but not in Spain."

"Well, what happened to those guys who lied to you about the work, El Jefe?" I asked.

He would always smile that gentle smile, then make a sad face and say, "Those people are no longer with us, I'm afraid."

That was my first conversation with him after I got to know him. Shavonda and the girl he was with had on the same Burberry bikini. That's how we got to talking on the beach.

I felt the getaway was much needed, with all this talk of Han being alive. Our flight was already scheduled. Patron was taking Lisa to pop bottles and relax. Shavonda was excited and hired some girl named Janet to run the All Goods Here store on the beach. We were all packed and set. Shavonda rolled over, kissed my shoulder, and then my neck.

"It's after three, baby, you okay?" she said, hair in a long ponytail, with matching Paradise bra and panties. Palm trees were the logo on the panties and bra. It was a bikini line she was doodling with. That's what I loved about Shavonda. She was always independent and smart. I was also down to invest in her ideas. "Another nightmare, baby?" she asked, pouting her lips sexily.

"Yeah, baby. Something like that," I said, laying back in the bed. We had five hours before our flight.

"Well," she said, kissing my chest, then my stomach. "Let me help you get back to sleep," Shavonda said before she devoured me. She was indeed talented and of course, after she was done, I was sound asleep.

The flight was wonderful because it was a private plane chartered only for the four of us, the pilot, co-pilot, and one stewardess who was more of a bartender.

Once the plane landed, Lisa and Patron, Shavonda and me headed to the Hotel Iturregi. I was told El Jefe was in France, which was only a day trip across the border, but he would be back before dark to say hello. I was always against consignment, but ten thousand a key of pink cocaine was so pure, I could make three bricks out of one. I was getting a hundred bricks all by myself. It would cost me a cool one million, but Patron had the other half. It's amazing how my life was in jeopardy a year ago over a hundred bricks I never got. Now I had a hundred bricks that was going to change the game.

I still got products from Wang, but never over twenty at a time. I still paid fifteen K's a brick, sometimes seventeen if shit was dry. Buying into El Jefe was every nigga's dream.

I felt like Ace when he met the connect by picking up his laundry in the movie *Paid in Full*. I was in all-white Gucci top and short with a white straw Gucci hat for the sun beaming with Gucci loafers, no socks. Patron had on an all-white Michael Kors shirt as well as shorts, with all-white Yeezy sneakers. Lisa and Shavonda had on all-white Fendi one pieces with matching Fendi scarves tied around their waists. We turned quite a few heads after getting situated with our luggage, then leaving the motel. Spain is a very sunny and beautiful place. Not bad for a twenty-three-year-old black orphan.

We stopped in the city of El Kano at a restaurant called Good Vibes. We ordered grilled fish, butter poached lobster, and Grey Goose. No ice for Patron and me. Shavonda was turning Lisa out on her favorite wine, Charles Woodson.

The restaurant had a dance floor with live music. All four of us danced and had a wonderful time. The natives taught us a dance that had us exhausted. The waiter came over and handed me a call phone.

"Hello," I said, feeling the Goose.

"Ah, my good friend, Yayo, how is Spain?" El Jefe asked.

"This is one classy country, El Jefe. I'm scared to wear sneakers, because even the waiters are dressed to kill," I said.

"Well, I am pleased you're pleased. I got the money transfer, so your gift is already in America. I'll be in Costa Brava in an hour. I already have transportation for you and your guests. May I ask, have you ever been in a castle?" he asked.

"A castle? Can't say I have. What exactly do you have in mind?" I said, trying to ignore Patron hitting me on the shoulder.

Patron interjected, "Yo dude got a castle, Oh, hell yeah!"

I shushed, then said, "No, but we would all love to see one."

"Well, Tossa De Mar has a fingernail of a beach booked by some low slum motels, but there is a twelfth-century castle that we throw some nice parties in. I'll see you there in an hour. Is this good?" El Jefe said.

"Yes, El Jefe, it's good," I said, then hung up. I waved for the waiter to come and get the phone. Once he came over, he said, "Sir, your ride awaits you to Costa Brava. On behalf of Spain, I hope you enjoy the sights." I tipped him a fifty-dollar bill after paying for our meal. Once outside, the big black diesel Benz awaited us.

"Damn, Terrence, are you and Yay in the mob or somethings?" Lisa asked, with not a clear clue of what we did to acquire the things we had.

"Baby, how come you can call Yay by his nickname, but not call me by my nickname?" Patron said as we all climbed in the Benz.

"Um, that's easy, Terrence, because you are my man and Yay is not. Neither of your moms gave you those names," Lisa said, but then the whole car was quiet. Neither Patron nor I knew our mothers. Once Lisa caught on, she seemed truly embarrassed.

"Oh, baby! Me and my mouth. Please, honey, forgive me," Lisa said, head down.

"Lisa, it's cool. We all family in here, and we are going to a castle. So, let's enjoy this time away from the city, okay?" Patron said, kissing Lisa on the forehead.

"Look, roll up some of that Purple we got in Spain, baby," Shavonda said kissing me on the cheek.

Once we pulled up, it was just getting a little dark. The castle was huge, and it rested on top of a cliff, with the beach below. It was the most beautiful thing I had ever seen in my life. The women were exotic, the men spoke different languages. Shit was fly!

A guy that looked like Harrison Ford opened the door of the Benz and said, "Welcome to Tossa De Mar. If you will please follow me. By the way, my name is Hector." We followed him up cobblestone steps that ran up the side of the cliff leading right into the castle. He spoke with an elegant voice. It seemed Hector was an educated man. He knew all of Spain, the restaurants and different islands to visit.

The castle had been in several *Dracula* movies in the 1940's. The rumor was a billionaire who fell in love with the island owned it. He left it for the public to enjoy. The parties occurred three times a week at the castle. Hector smiled and said, "You came just in time. Tonight is the first party of the week."

All nationalities were present. Spanish, Mexican, Honduran, black, white, and even a guy who had flown in from Russia, just for the party of all parties. At least that is what he said. The castle was huge, but there were certain areas that were off limits. This was to keep the party tamed. Long candles were everywhere, a live rock-n-roll band played songs from Jimmy Hendrix and Bob Marley. We were brought into a huge room with a sunken pool in the middle of the floor.

El Jefe was sitting with no less than twenty exotic looking women. Bodyguards in every corner and shadow of the room. He got up to approach me. Patron said, "Damn, El Jefe! Look just like Robert De Niro, man. How crazy is that?"

I couldn't lie. He looked exactly like De Niro, but the gangsters Robert played were the real thing for this guy. If you crossed him, he would wipe out your whole bloodline.

He embraced me. "Yayo, my friend, so how do you like the castle? Not only that, but he whispered in my ear, "All the women love foreign men. Too bad you brought sand to the beach." He pulled back from the embrace and laughed.

"I'm good, El Jefe. I got me a good one," I said.

"Well, you better hold on to her. These girls, they remember my money. Not me," he said.

I called everyone over to introduce them. "This is my brother, Patron," I said as they shook hands. "Also, his girlfriend, Lisa. And this is my baby, Shavonda." He shook their hands.

"Ah yes, Shavonda, she is beautiful. I guess there is no sand worthy in this beach. Anyway, I have an engagement. Enjoy yourselves, and Yayo, call me as soon as you are back in the States." He winked and then was gone with Hector and an entourage of females in tow.

I got glasses for all of us and a gold bottle, which was a gift from El Jefe. I poured the gold liquid in everyone's glass and raised mine. "To a new life, new beginning, and I'm glad all of you are here," I said as we all tapped our glasses.

"And I would like to give a toast to Robert de Niro because Spain is the shit!" said Patron as we all laughed. I hugged Patron.

"Broke niggas make noise," I said.

"And rich niggas make moves," Patron said.

We danced all night. The castle was packed. Lisa flipped on some Cuban girl she thought was eyeing Patron. We laughed when we found out the girl was a lesbian and was really trying to hit on Lisa.

Everyone gets that feeling. You know? The feeling that things are too good to be true. I was getting money, real money. We lost Polo and Laylow along the way, but we were still breathing and that is always good. For some reason, the guy in the green Izod shirt and white pants caught my eye. Was this the third time he had walked by? The shades on his face didn't stop me from feeling I knew this guy. Then it hit me like a ton of bricks.

Lisa and Shavonda were dancing off a Sade song, "Smooth Operator" was blaring through the speakers. I walked over to Patron and whispered in his ear, "Yo, you strapped?"

Patron looked at me. "Does Kim Kardashian have a big ass? Of course, I am strapped, homie. We took a chartered plane. Why, what's wrong?" Patron asked, scanning the room.

"You see the fool talking to the big Puerto Rican that looks like The Rock?" I asked.

"Oh, shit. Yay, you got to be kidding me. What the hell they doing in Spain?" Patron said, his hand under his Michael Kors shirt.

I couldn't believe it either. It was Felipe in the green Izod shirt and white pants. He was talking to Esteban, who was wearing a pink Izod shirt, white pants and white loafers. There were two other men with them, and they were all looking our way.

I said, "We got to get the girls out of here. Then we will have to figure it out as we go," as Hector walked into the room. I walked up to him and said, "Hector, I need you to please escort the ladies back to the Hotel Iturregi, if you please." I gave him two hundred-dollar-bills. He only nodded as I approached the girls. "I need for both of you to go with Hector right now. We will meet you in about an hour." They could tell something was wrong.

"Yay, what is going on?" Shavonda said.

"Terrence, why are we leaving you two around all these foreign hoes?" Lisa said, words slurring.

Patron walked up to Lisa, kissed her, looked at Shavonda and said, "Get the fuck out of here, please."

I guess it was the way Patron said it. They were both walking out the door with Hector. There was a beam on Patron. I pushed him just as the gun went off. *BOOM, BOOM*

The DJ caught two to the chest. Everyone was screaming and running in different directions. Total chaos had broken out. I raised my Desert Eagle out of my Gucci pants. *BOOM, BOOM, BOOM, BOOM* I gave a head shot to one of the guys with Felipe. Patron squatted behind a sofa, popping his nine. *BOOM, BOOM, BOOM* Another guy grabbed his leg, yelling out in pain.

"Oh, my God! Yay, baby!" Shavonda yelled, with Hector holding her back.

"Get the hell out of here! Hector, get them out of here!" I yelled.

All three of them were running, rushing out with a crowd of people. I slid beside Patron, and I could see he was hit in the foot.

"I'm going to kill them motherfuckers. I just bought these fucking Yeezy's, man," Patron said, popping a few shots off in Felipe and Esteban's direction.

BOOM, BOOM, BOOM "Yay, you slimy son of a bitch!" Felipe said as he shot toward us. "You owe me twenty-five keys, my friend." *BOOM, BOOM*

"You made a fool out of me, and now I'm at war with the Italians!" yelled Esteban. "It is the date you die today." *BOOM, BOOM, BOOM*

They had us pinned behind a huge couch, and a few of the partygoers were hiding or on the floor with their heads down. I felt something hit me on my side. At first, I thought I was hit, but it was the Cristal bottle rolling beside me. I ripped off a piece of my shirt and stuffed it in the bottle. Patron looked at me and nodded his understanding.

"Fuck you, Felipe! You child molesting piece of shit! Your aim is as bad as your choice in women. Oops! I meant little girls," I yelled to piss off Felipe off. I could see Esteban's shadow creeping near Patron's side. I counted shots. It was a habit. Felipe only had three shots left before he had to reload. I was not quite sure about Esteban. I just knew Felipe was the closest.

"Fuck you, Yay! I kill you and your nigga friend." *BOOM, BOOM, BOOM, CLICK, CLICK* Then I heard him trying to reload, and it was my chance.

I lit the cloth on the bottle then hurled it towards Felipe. Patron raised up and let out every shot at Esteban. I raised my gun and aimed it at the bottle as best I could. *BOOM, BOOM, BOOM, BOOM* The bottle burst into flames. Felipe was getting barbecued. The smell of burnt flesh was putrid and suffocating in the castle. Esteban took one to the shoulder while running toward Felipe. It was too late. He let out a wild scream and pointed the gun at Patron. I pointed my gun and pulled the trigger. *CLICK, CLICK*

Esteban laughed, "You take my brother, and now I take yours," he said, blood gushing from his shoulder.

Then out of nowhere, the room was filled with armed men. Some had AK-47's and some AR-15's. There was a guy with a fire extinguisher putting what was left of Felipe out. I thought they were Esteban's men, but they had the guns pointed at Esteban, Patron, and me. The two guys with Esteban and Felipe were dead. One died instantly. The other bled out from a bad leg wound. Esteban stared hard at Patron, then me, and then he dropped his gun. We were all taken to a room in a different part of the castle. Once we were in the room, El Jefe was leaning against the wall. Hector rapidly talking in his ear.

"I don't care about the businesses of men who want to kill each other. However, the sanctity of a twelfth-century castle has been tainted. There hasn't been violence in this part of the world since Ivan the Terrible. So, I will ask one time. Who killed my DJ?" El Jefe said, looking at all of us.

"My apologies, El Jefe. I was only trying to protect my fiancée and my brother's girlfriend. Nothing more," I said.

"This piece of shit killed my brother!" Esteban yelled.

"Silence!" El Jefe yelled. "Hector told me as he was escorting the girls out, you," El Jefe said, pointing a finger at Esteban, then pushing his finger into Esteban's bullet hole. Esteban's screams filled the room. "Pulled your gun in the party like some common gangbanger at a drive-by." He then wiped his finger on Esteban's pink Izod shirt. "Your impatience to take someone's life was your mistake. I don't care who wants to kill whom, as long as it is not done in the presence of my guests. DJ Fusion played a lot of Justin Bieber."

Then El Jefe pulled out a .45 Glock with a silencer on it. *Poof, Poof* two shots straight to Esteban's head. "I like Justin Bieber," he said and then looked to his men. "Get the both of them cleaned up." Then he walked towards me as Hector and another of his men were helping Patron to his feet.

"Yay, this will not happen again. You already have a hundred keys in the States. No more of this foolishness, my young one."

"I'm sorry, El Jefe. I didn't know this would happen," I said.

"Well, a man makes his own choices and accepts the outcome as his karma. Just be glad you weren't the one what killed the DJ, and also that you have business in play." He winked at me and was gone.

I knew things had to change because he politely let me know, the only reason I was not dead was because the keys were already in the States. Lucky for me!

Fre$h

Chapter 5

In One Piece...

We were dropped off at the hotel a good hour later. Hector, riding shotgun in the all-black Audi, made it clear how things were. "El Jefe knows those men started the shooting. If not for that, and you had started this issue, it would be your bodies fed to the sharks. Anyway, your chartered flight leaves first thing in the morning. Good luck to you, gentlemen," Hector said as he and the driver drove off.

I felt relieved, tired, and still glad we made it through another day. Patron had crutches and a private doctor fixed him up. I had been looked over and small pieces of glass had been removed from my face, as well as my arms. When the bottle exploded, chards hit me, but I didn't notice until after the fact.

When I swiped my card to the hotel room, the girls looked as if they would pass out. My Gucci outfit was stained with mine and Patron's blood. Patron's pants were ripped where they worked on his foot. My shirt was ripped where I had made the homemade cocktail out of the bottle. Patron was on pain pills, and so was I. Shavonda walked up to us, and we both flopped down in two chairs by a table near the AC unit by the window. I know we looked a mess, but we were alive. Lisa was sitting on the bed, mouth wide open, but no words came out.

"Hey, um, honey could you look in the table drawer and get the Garcia Vega out?" I said as I dug in my pockets for the eighth of Purple Haze I had left. She just nodded nervously and brought me the box. My hip was hurting, and I realized the Desert Eagle was rubbing my hip raw. I pulled it out and set it on the table, pointing it towards the window. Patron leaned his crutches against the wall and pulled out his nine, pointing it towards the window.

"Man, roll a big ass blunt, fam," Patron said.

"I'm way ahead of you, playa. Damn, them fools really tried to end us," I said, rolling damn near all the Purple.

"Yeah, but let Hector tell it, the sharks getting they *Jaws* on. Damn, a shootout in Spain. Who the hell going to believe that?" Patron said, propping his foot in another chair opposite him.

"Shit, I don't believe it! Let Hector tell it, when you were getting patched up, some Italian man ran them out of there selling that work Shitty Smitty whipped up. Word is they were looking for a new connect. Guess I beat them to it," I said lighting the blunt.

"Well, either you got a four-leaf clover in your ass or someone praying for us. Oh, and you owe me a pair of Yeezy sneakers," Patron said, looking through the hole.

"Hey, sweetheart, can you get that Grey Goose out the mini fridge?" Patron said as I passed him the blunt. Lisa came over, put the bottle down, and we both took thirsty swigs of what Young Jeezy calls clear liquid Holy Water.

Lisa and Shavonda were both standing in their matching Fendi bikinis, arms crossed, looking at us like we were crazy.

"Are you two out of your damn minds? We were worried sick. Terrence, baby, you have a hole in your foot!" Lisa yelled.

"And Yay, you look like you had a fight with bottles of glass and lost," Shavonda said pouting.

"Baby, listen, it was an issue at the Castle and some guys started shooting up the place. Yay and I wanted to make sure both of you were safe. We both made it out, those other fools didn't, and that's all that matters," Patron said, kissing Lisa's forehead as she hugged him while he was sitting.

"Vonda, I know it may be a lot of things you don't know. But honey, the less you know, the safer you will be. But I love you, and your safety is my number-one priority. Soon both of us," I glanced at Patron. "Will be done with a lot of these um, let's just call it, unfortunate activities," I said, getting up and hugging her. "I love you, girl."

Wiping her eyes and hugging me, she said, "I love you too, Yay, just don't ever scare me like that again. Okay?"

"Okay, I got you, man. No worries," I said.

"Well, Lisa, if you can accept me all beat up and shot up, I hope you can accept what I ask of you next," Patron said, digging in his pants pocket.

"What, Terrence? Are you about to admit you are a terrorist now?" She started to grin, but worry was on her face.

"Not at all, baby, but if I could get on one knee, I would. So, I'll ask you this sitting down, baby. Will you marry me?" Patron said, pulling out a box with a ring made by Harry Winston, with crushed diamonds shaped like lips on a thick gold band. It was custom-made, so I know it cost Patron a grip. Lisa was speechless and mumbling all kinds of things Shavonda nor I could understand.

"Girl, please, just say yes. If that's what you're trying to say," Shavonda said, beaming with joy for her friend.

"Oh my God, baby! Yes, yes, yes!" Lisa said, grabbing Patron almost knocking him down. "Oh, baby, your foot! But yes, boy, I'll marry you!"

Shavonda smiled at them, then came and sat on my lap. She kissed me in the places the glass had cut me. It was only a few spots. My arm got most of it. It stung, but I'd live.

"Baby, are we okay? I mean, I don't want to lose you, but it is what it is. I told you once I know everything's everything, I'm out," I said.

"Promise, baby?" Shavonda asked with that big booty on my lap.

"That's a promise, girl. As a matter of fact, I didn't know my brother was going to pop the question, but I felt it. This drama tonight lets me know life is short. So, I need you to look in your Prada bag," I said, smiling my gold grill smile.

"But baby, I got on Fendi, so I only have my Fendi purse out. You got me... you know... you told me never mix designer," Shavonda said, getting off my lap.

"Go to your suitcase and look in your Prada bag," I said as I watched her hips shake back and forth as she made her way to the suitcase. Then from the bedroom we heard a loud scream. I just shrugged my shoulders at Lisa and Patron as they were looking at me. Then Shavonda walked from the bedroom to the table we were all sitting at, carrying a big box.

I got up and made her sit in the chair I was sitting in. Then I took the box from her hands, and I got on one knee.

"Okay, family. I see you, big bruh," Patron said, cheering me on.

I looked in Shavonda's eyes. "I've been through some shit. By the standard of The Evils as Jay-Z said, I should be dead going on three times." I thought about the Russians, then Han kidnapping me, and then tonight. "But baby, I'm still here. You been down, you opened your home to me and your heart. So, I'm asking you, will you be Mrs. Baxter?" I opened up the box, and Shavonda almost fainted. It was a ring, a big ring made by Van Cleef & Arpels, 1906 model with rubies and diamonds, mounted on a platinum band.

I even bought a necklace to match it, which would be finished when we got back to the States. I bought it a few days after Wang and Fujj's visit. She handled that situation like a G. Therefore, she was wifey material.

Shavonda was babbling something to me and blinking her eyes all crazy as I slipped it on her perfectly manicured finger.

Lisa laughed at her and only repeated what Shavonda had said just minutes before. "Girl, please just say yes, if that's what you're trying to say," Lisa said smiling, still hugged up sitting beside Patron.

"Hell yes, I'll marry you!" Shavonda said, hugging me as she jumped out the chair.

Patron had four plastic cups on the table. He poured Grey Goose in each cup, and we all picked one up.

"I now pronounce everyone in this room my family, because I never had one. To my brother and now my sister," Patron said, nodding at Shavonda. "Now, you two are sisters. Love every day like the next day may not come," Patron said as we all tapped our plastic cups together.

"Rich niggas make moves," Patron said to me across the table, passing me the blunt of Purple.

"While broke niggas make noise," I said, feeling we had ducked another day of drama. Our rooms were connected, so Shavonda and I gave Patron and Lisa privacy. The bathtub was huge because we both had suites at the hotel. Shavonda bathed me, then helped me out the bath and even dried me off. As I lay on the bed with nothing but a towel on, I heard the music begin to play, and I knew it was Prince. Shavonda was thirty years old, even though I was twenty-three going on twenty-four. We both loved some Prince though. "Until the end of time, I'll be there for you," Prince sang.

Shavonda walked up to the bed with only a yellow thong on, tits plump and staring at me. I felt like I'd died because the vibe we had was heaven. She kissed my toes one by one, and moved up, kissing my thighs while looking deep in my eyes, lust filling hers. I was so hard the towel looked like an Indian tent.

"Mmmm," she purred in her sexy voice, still looking at me with dark desire in her eyes. "Is that for me?" she asked, her eyes cutting to the towel. Before I could even respond, she took me in her mouth and deep throated me. I tried to lean up, but she shoved me back down.

She stood up over me as she tossed the towel to the side and turned her big ass to face me. There was a mirror over us and a big one beside the bed. The reflection made it look like there were three of us. She pulled her thong to the side and lowered her wetness on my dick. Her hands were on my knees, balancing her weight.

"Yes, daddy! Beat this pussy, it's all yours, baby." She moaned and purred, her big ass slapping my thighs sounding like thunder clapping. I grabbed her ass and slammed her down violently on my manhood. Han, Wang and Fujj all far from my mind. Only thing I was focused on was Shavonda bouncing on me.

Chapter 6

Turn Up!

We slept a majority of the flight back. Patron was off with Lisa to see a foot doctor. It felt so good to be back in VA. Even though Spain was fly, the run-in with Felipe and Esteban pretty much ruined that. I had a few voice messages from Milk Marie, reminding me I had a son, and I could have told her I was going out of town. Shavonda let it slip to her that we were in Spain.

But you know females. I don't need a lock on my phone. The text she sent Milk Marie from Spain said, "I'll tell him you called." I guess she felt some type of way. Shavonda went back to her shop, and she ended up firing the helper she had. She hired a young white boy named Chase, and she said he was picking up fast.

I took a day to meditate and get my head right. The shootout in Spain had me on edge. I watched *The Godfather* and just tried to relax. I looked at my phone, and there was a text from Milk Marie.

"Can you talk or are you still away on business?" she asked.

I shook my head and called her phone. "Yo, what's up? How is my son?" I said, putting out the blunt and turning down the TV. Al Pacino had just kissed Fredo, telling him he knew he had set him up.

"What's up is Wang is trying to get us to go to Atlanta in a few days. He is beyond focused on this Ken Chew dude. Oh, and Malcolm is fine if you must know. I'm actually about to get off work. Malcolm is in daycare." The phone was quiet for a few beats. She said, "You didn't have to pay for the daycare. I can manage, Yay," she said with attitude.

"Look, regardless of the issues between us, I love my son. I want to give him all I didn't have," I said, rolling another blunt.

"I feel you, but the daycare is paid up until he is five years old. He is only sixteen weeks, Yay," she said with less attitude.

"Hey, kids grow up fast," I said.

"You're an asshole, Yay."

"But I am still a good dad and great provider," I retorted.

"Look, I know your feelings or whatever, have changed for me. I don't want our son involved in that life."

"Girl, bye. I'll do whatever is necessary for mine. Believe that! Better than your other sperm donors do," I said, regretting the remark.

"For real, Yay? You're going to go there? I work, and I do my best. My past is my past."

"Well, be careful, the past is known to haunt you."

"Only thing is, you won't let the past go." Then the line was quiet. "Someone bought my kids a year's worth of shoes, clothes, and Xbox games. My mom said it all showed up at the house a month ago."

"Look to me, it's a blessing. I bet they all like the different pairs of Jordans."

"I never said what kind of shoes they were, Yay." She laughed, but I still never admitted to being the one who'd sent the gifts. "Anyway, how was Spain?" she asked sarcastically.

"Good and bad, I suppose. Patron and me bumped into Felipe and his big ass brother, Esteban," I said, lighting another blunt.

"Oh shit, the guys Shitty Smitty got for the—" I cut her off before she could finish.

"Yeah, yeah, the guys that got-got. Anyway, Patron got shot in the foot, and I got some bruises and a little broken glass on me. But everything good though," I said, still seeing Felipe's body burst into flames.

"So, what happened to Felipe and Esteban?" she said, with Cardi B playing in the background.

"Oh, shit, them niggas went to go see Elvis," I said laughing, "blue suede shoes and all."

"See, Yay, that's what I don't want Malcolm in the middle of. Anyway, Wang said in a couple of days he will contact you. To be honest, I'm a little scared."

"Shit, you should be, shorty. Anyway, this the Chinese Triad. We just possibly going to see how many of Wang and Fujj's toes Ken Chew stepped on. Then we out. Why did you volunteer?" I paused. "Well, you know that warehouse situation." I could still see Milk Marie trembling as Hans made me point the Colt 45 at her.

"Because that pussy was going to push you to kill me, then probably kill you anyway. While you were unconscious, I heard Han flipping out about you, Laylow, and Polo killing two Russians. Well, if that bastard is still alive, I'm serving his eggroll eating ass on a silver platter. But, if Wang is just paranoid, then I get closer," Milk Marie said.

"Yeah, I can't lie, I'm just trying to kill my curiosity. Either way, after all this is done, I'm done. Fuck Elizabeth City. I am going to Rio for a year, but Virginia Beach I still love," I said, checking out the view from the front window, looking out to the strip, which was connected to the beach.

Is that why you moved out here?" she said.

"Look, I had no idea you had an apartment out here until seven months after I had already left E-City Towers. I told you to keep the apartment in Hemington Village."

"Fuck you. You and Patron old cook spot. No thank you."

"Watch the attitude, because that was even before I knew you and Han..." I didn't finish my sentence.

"Yay, look, I didn't mean…" Milk Marie said but never finished.

"Check it, I got to go. Fed Ex is ringing the doorbell. Listen, there is a spot over on Ocean View. I want my son in a good spot. After all this is over, it's up to you if you want it. Tell yuh mom what's up. I'm off this," I said and hung up, then tossed the phone on the coffee table to answer the door. There was a police officer with the Fed Ex guy. I opened the door.

"Yes sir, is there one Seemiyun Baxter here?" he asked.

"Yeah, that's me," I replied.

"Sir, I need to see your ID, then sign where the X is on the paper this young man has for you." I did what I was told and signed. They left me with a pink box with a big yellow bow. I opened it and there was the necklace that matched Shavonda's ring. It was a Zip Antique Ludo necklace and had matching rubies and diamonds, just like the ring. The necklace could even turn into a bracelet. Damn near sixty thousand altogether, but loyalty is priceless. Plus, Shavonda was a loyal dime, and I had planned to spoil her like old Milk.

I put everything back in the box, waiting to surprise Shavonda later. Then my phone's ring tone was playing, "Young savage why you trippin so hard/Why you pulling all these rappers cards/Because they soft and I'm hard/I turn some soft in to some hard…"

"Yo, what's really good?" I answered.

"Hey, um, this James—James Richards, Yay. Uh, I just signed for a load of mulch for you. Are you coming by to get it?" See, James was paying the fee to Patron, though we were splitting it. I had my stuff coming through James' Lawn Care Service. I would even let him have some mulch for side jobs, because we were damn near draining him. Shit, after Patron kidnapped him and damn near killed him, he didn't give a damn. Even tried to sell me the business, but even though it was doing well, I declined. I didn't want no type of connection with James. He was a piece of shit, but for now, a useful piece of shit.

"I'll have my guys come pick it up in less than an hour. The soft mulch is yours, the package marked brown mulch is mine," I said.

"Cool, Yay. Thanks, man. I…" James tried to reply, but I hung up on him. The guy was a lowlife. I made a note to change the dropoff after a few more loads.

I had met two stick-up kids boosting cars out of Virginia. These guys weren't taking Mazda or Honda, not even close. They were stealing Porsche, Benz, Lexus, and the like. I was walking toward my Lamborghini Aventador that I always parked a block from our home in Virginia Beach. As I approached the boardwalk, a short, brown-skinned bald dude with glasses was trying to pry my door up. I reached for my gun, but a boardwalk officer was already approaching him.

"Excuse me, sir. Is this your vehicle?" the boardwalk officer said with reflective shades on.

"Honestly, sir, it's my cousin's car. I've never drove it. I feel dumb. I don't know how to lift the doors," he replied to the officer.

I shook my head because I could tell the cop wasn't buying it. Because for my model Lamborghini, you needed the push button key for the door to go up. Unless you were already in the vehicle, then you could open it from the inside. I decided to step in.

"Young man, I think I need to see some ID," the officer said, stepping toward the guy who was trying to steal my car.

"That won't be necessary, Officer, my knucklehead cousin forgot the keys," I said, producing my keys, driver's license, and proof the car was mine.

"Okay. It all checks out, but you guys be careful out here with these nice cars. We got a tip it's two guys stealing cars around the beach strip. Hell, one even posed as a valet at the Hilton and drove off with a Porsche," the officer said as he strolled off toward the boardwalk.

"I'll keep that in mind, Officer. Thank you," I said. Once the officer was gone, I introduced myself.

"What's my name? Yay. This is my car you were trying to steal. It works better with the key, homie," I said, holding up the keys. "So, what's your name? I figure you owe me since Barney Fife was about to jail you."

"My name is Pierre, Pierre Lunggington, and I didn't need your key." Then Pierre popped the doors up, showing me he knew what he was doing.

"Okay, have to talk to the dealer that sold me this fine machine. So do you want a job, Pierre?" I said.

"My friends call me P-Funk, and why you want to give me a job? I just tried to steal your car," he said shocked.

"Well, if the cop didn't get you," I flashed my Desert Eagle in the waistline of my Levi's, "Betsy here would have got you. Plus, from the sound of it, the authorities are on to you. But the real question is, where is your partner?" I said, looking around. Patron and me used to steal when we were still at the orphanage. Patron was my lookout, and the cops did say there were two guys suspected of stealing cars. P-Funk looked at me for a few seconds, thinking.

"Look, let's just say I didn't always drive a Lamborghini," I said, showing my gold-toothed grin. P-Funk seemed convinced. Then he let out a loud whistle and leaned on my car.

"If you're serious, you got to take my boy too," P-Funk said as a young black guy, who was sitting on a bench pretending to read a newspaper, approached us. His hair was in braids. He had on a white tee, shorts and Jordans on his feet. He had tattoos all over his face.

"Yo, P-Funk, I thought we were going to have to roll on Po-Po. Who the fuck is this dude?" the guy said with street attitude. In my mind, they were both perfect for my team.

"This the nigga's car, and he saved my ass from the flashlight boardwalk cop. Excuse my friend. This is Rasheed, AKA Gucci Swag," P-Funk said.

"That's Swagg with two G's. So, this your ride? What, you a rapper or something?" Gucci Swagg said, looking me up and down.

"No, I'm not a rapper, but I got a lot them thangs that need to be wrapped, feel me? So, yuh mans said he not down without you." I looked at my Cartier watch. "Look, I got some things to handle. You making a little dough with the car shit, but you two are hot. Today proved that, so fuck that *Fast & Furious* shit. You two down?" I said, lifting the door up.

"What we got to do?" Gucci Swagg asked.

"Shit what you been doing. Driving. Pick up and drop off. That's it," I said, getting in my car.

"I'm down, my dude. When do we start?" P-Funk said.

"Today," I said to both of them.

"Shit, homie. Turn up then," Gucci Swagg said.

They been down ever since. I gave P-Funk a call while putting Shavonda's present up.

"My nigga, Yayo. What up, homie?" P-Funk said.

"Yo, I need you and Gucci Swagg to pick up at James' Lawn Care Service. Take the mulch to Patron and tell him I'll be to him in an hour," I said.

"Say no more, big homie, we on the way," P-Funk said in the driver's seat of his all-black F-150. Gucci Swagg had a matching dark green one, but the two always traveled together.

Niggas knew not to fuck with Gucci Swagg or P-Funk. Their body count was retarded. The guy they used to boost cars for, come to find out, was ripping them off. They were his best car thieves. All of a sudden, no one ever heard from or saw that dude again. Now, the two of them were running the chop shop out of Richmond. I never got into their affairs, but everyone was eating. The first time I paid the two of them for transporting, they told me it would take stealing seven cars to get that amount. Then my phone started buzzing. I must have turned it down after talking to Milk Marie.

"Yo, what up?" I said.

"Yayo, what's good, baby boy?" Patron said.

"What's up, bruh? How's the foot?" I said, rolling some Purple up.

"I'm good. It went straight through. That doctor El Jefe had on deck was official. My personal doctor got an attitude after seeing me wrapped up so professionally. Can you believe these white people? I'm sitting in his office with a hole in my foot, and this Doogie Howser looking dude worried somebody else eating off my injury," Patron said frustrated.

"Patron, it's called business. Why you think he referred you to the foot doctor? They both going to get a piece. Feel me?" I said, inhaling the Purple I lit.

"Business or not, I still want a new pair of Yeezy's. Anyway, you hit Shavonda with the part two of the engagement ring yet?" Patron said whispering, not wanting Lisa to overhear.

"Not yet, but since you just getting in from the doctor, them thangs coming your way," I said, hearing the door open. I knew my girl, Shavonda, was coming home to take lunch.

"Damn, El Jefe a beast. How does he do it?" Patron said in awe.

"I don't know. This is our first hundred, so let's get this money. Gucci Swagg and P-Funk on they way to your sporting goods spot. I'll be there in a few," I said.

"Okay. That's a bet. Can still drive. Lisa is on her way to get a manicure and pedicure. So, I'm good," Patron said.

"No doubt, my G. See you in a few. Broke niggas make noise," I said.

"And rich niggas make moves," Patron replied.

Once I hung the phone up, I watched Shavonda walk into the living room. The sun's rays from outside made the rock on her hand gleam from all over the room like a disco ball. Her long ponytail was down her back. She had on a two-hundred-dollar palm-print Norma Kamali jumpsuit, with four-hundred-dollar Saint Laurent Aviator sunglasses, and an emerald Hermes Birkin bag. Shavonda looked like a damn runway model instead of the boss over All Goods Here Store on the strip. She got the Birkin bag in Spain, before all hell broke loose, of course.

"Hey, baby. I didn't think you would be home today. Everything okay?" she said, coming over and kissing me, and giving me a big hug.

"I'm good, just got to handle something with Patron today," I said, putting the remote to the TV on top of the huge pink box with the yellow bow on it. I yawned, acting like I was paying the box no mind. I passed her the blunt and she was hitting it, eyeing the box. She put her shades on the coffee table.

"Um, baby, what's this?" she said, fanning the smoke.

"I don't know. Fed Ex delivered it. I figured it was something you ordered," I said, trying to hold in my laugh. She passed me back the blunt, and I stood at the kitchen door watching her open it.

"Holy shit, holy shit! Oh my God, Yay, this necklace matches my ring! Aww!" she screamed, grabbing me and hugging me.

"Well, with all that was going on in Spain, I couldn't get it until once we were back in the States. I love you, girl," I said, smiling at her. "Here. Let me put it on for you," I said, putting the expensive necklace around her neck as she looked in the living room mirror. My phone buzzed again. "Yeah?" I answered.

"We just dropped that mulch off to Patron," Gucci Swagg said.

"Okay, cool. I'll have both of your fees by tonight," I said.

"Say no more, homie. See you then. One," Gucci Swagg said.

"One," I replied, then I hung up the phone and turned around. Shavonda was naked, with only the ring and necklace on. She pulled me to the couch and pulled my Hilfiger jeans off.

"Baby, I got to handle something," I said, feeling her mouth on me.

"Shut up and enjoy, daddy," she said, swallowing me.

"Damn! Turn up then," I said, leaning back, hands in Shavonda's hair.

Chapter 7

Money Over Everything...

After Shavonda tried to pull my dick off my body, we hit the streets hard with the product El Jefe gave us. Shit was going like hot cakes. See, networking is to meet new people. But people who are in the life hide it well. That was the key to drug dealing. I know a guy that owned a store that bought at least two bricks from me. Another guy who used to do films was John Singleton's apprentice. Now he was getting money by directing pornos, starring himself of course. Cashed in, now he gets five keys from me, and has his own porno website company called Wet Adventures. Patron was also making a killing. He sent his share to El Jefe after the foot doctor appointment.

I was riding through the strip, windows halfway down, feeling the breeze in my Lamborghini. A hundred bricks almost ruined my life and got people killed. But me and Patron were truly eating. It was a nice day, and I was pulling up to a Starbucks. I had on an all-brown Gucci jumpsuit, with gold trim and brown Gucci Jordans I had preordered from a show dealer in Taiwan. Gucci shades on with my favorite Prada cologne, dreads in a ponytail, chillin. The line was a little long, but it was cool. I was in a good mood.

There was this beautiful woman a few places in front of me in line. I could have sworn I had seen her before. She looked like an older version of Taylor Swift, the singer, but her tan made her have an olive complexion. Her eyes were gray, like thunderclouds right before the rain. Her hair fell in layers down both sides of her face. The dress she wore was a Givenchy frock. Black and white designs, it came right above her knees. Her back and white Givenchy high heels made her legs look broad. She had a necklace with Jesus on the cross, it was rose gold. She must have felt me staring at her. She looked back at me and in a sexy, flirtatious voice said, "Well, hello, my dear baby daddy." Maybe it was just my imagination.

"Um, do we know each other?" I said, enjoying her perfume.

"I picked Milk Marie up a while back. I'm Vicky, but my friends call me Victoria," she said, smiling at me. "You here to get a latte or something, Mr. Yay?" She looked through me with those piercing gray eyes.

"How you seem to know me, but I don't know you?" I said, trying not to pay attention to her curves. I've seen my share of women, but Victoria was beautiful.

"Well, I go in the Peabody like three times a week, and Milk Marie makes sure I get extra liquor in my Long Island Iced Tea. You have a little boy named Malcolm, and from the looks of her life, she regrets something she did," Victoria said, moving up in line.

"Well, it just didn't work, but that's another story." I started sniffing again. "You smell wonderful, if I do say so."

"Your senses are that good in a coffee shop? Well, if you tell me what perfume I am wearing, I will buy your latte," she said, waving her scent from her neck. Yes, we were flirting, and I couldn't help it. She was so witty.

"Okay, um, it's definitely Dior and as a matter of fact, it's Joy by Dior," I said, knowing I was right.

"How did you do that?" Then she looked me up and down. "Well, a man dressed in all Gucci I'm sure has bought plenty of perfume for plenty of women," she said as we got to the counter for me to collect my prize.

"Well, not really. See, my boy Patron's fiancée loves Jennifer Lawrence and she, I think, promotes Dior. So, whenever she comes over with him, she wears it." I pointed at my nose.

"I have a good nose and a good eye. Oh, I would like a Frappuccino with extra caramel, not a latte."

"Well, I thought I was bougie, but I do like the Prada you have on," she said as she got my drink and hers from the counter. I took my drink from her hand and walked her outside.

"Sounds like I'm not the only one who has a nose," I said, leaning on my car.

"Honestly, I have two boys, twins actually. I gave one of them the same cologne."

"Small world," I said, sipping my drink.

"Indeed, it is."

"What exactly do your twin boys do?" I asked.

"Oh, they are part of a clean-up crew. They travel and pretty much stay busy. I'm only down here on business, love. We are from England, my parents moved to Maryland. Now, I am a fashion agent," she said smiling. I had walked her to her Jaguar, not even realizing it.

"I thought you owned a Jeep," I said.

"No, I'm into foreigns. That was one of my twins' car. I'm guessing there is a lady in your life."

"Yes. Yes, there is, and I'm sure there is someone in yours," I said, still looking at how gorgeous she was.

"There was, but I cut his head off, and that is quite a long story." She then gave me a kiss on the cheek. Her lips were soft, and the Joy by Dior was in my nostrils. She got in her car and made a tsk, tsk noise shaking her head. "Always the good ones already taken."

I had never even thought of another woman since I met Shavonda, but Victoria was exotic. I couldn't lie. She turned me on.

"Well, at least you're honest," she said, rolling her window down.

"Um, you never told me what your business was you were down here for," I said, hating our flirting was coming to an end.

"My business, Yay, if you must know, was to see an old friend off. He passed away recently. I may stay around a while." She looked me up and down. "I like the view around here.

"I'm sorry your old friend, as you say, passed away. What was his name?" I said, knowing she was staring at the bulge in my Gucci jumpsuit. She slid her shades on and started her Jag.

She said to me sadly, "His name was Han Che." She winked at me, pulled her shades all the way up, and drove off. *How the hell did she know Han Che? And how did I miss her at the funeral, beautiful as she was? Probably because me and Patron left early. I bet Han Che probably banged her. Oh well.* I walked to my car and then my phone rang.

"What up, Patron? You running up a check or what?" I said, still watching Victoria drive away in her Jag. You could tell she had money. I tried not to let it bother me that she knew Han Che, but it did.

"We got a problem, homie. Gucci Swagg shot the nigga Tyrone from Belmont Avenue," Patron said irritated.

"You telling me the same Tyrone owed me for three keys? Where you at now?" I said, knowing in the streets there is no such things as a normal day.

"I'm at the cookhouse in Herrington Village. Pierre is on his way with Gucci Swagg right now," Patron said, cocking his gun.

"Bet. I'm on the way," I said.

"Say no more," Patron said, hanging up.

I went to surprise Shavonda at the shop, and she was showing off her ring to a girl named Princess she had not long hired.

The other guy got a managing position at the Hilton, but she pretty much told me Princess always wanted a shop as well.

Princess was from Newport News and dark-skinned, with pretty chocolate skin. She favored Gabrielle Union, but I could see why Shavonda liked her. She had on a Fendi jogging suit that fit her just right around her thick figure. Even wore a Fendi headband which kept her long, Indian textured hair falling down her back. I brought them some doughnuts and told Shavonda I needed to drive her BMW. I gave her my keys and got hers out of her office.

The shop was filled with bracelets with sewn-on names, and t-shirts with unicorns, tank tops and mugs with *Virginia is For Lovers* on them. She gave me a funny look as Princess went to stock some shades on the far wall.

"Boy, you never let me drive the Lambo. What's going on, Yay?" she whispered as the bell rang, signaling a customer had walked in.

"Nothing wrong, baby. I'm going in town, and I don't like taking the Lambo out that way," I said, kissing her on the cheek, leaving.

"I get to keep it all day?" she yelled to my back. I just threw my hands up. I knew soon as I left, she was going to drive it. Didn't matter, I just didn't want a two-hundred-thousand-dollar car in the projects.

Once I got there, I parked beside Pierre's F-150. Patron's all-black Lexus was parked a few spaces down. I checked my gun, then put it in my waistband, took the stairs two at a time. I used my key for the apartment me and Patron kept when we really first started out. I heard arguing soon as I came in.

"In broad daylight? Fuck is wrong with you, Gucci Swagg? Better hope nobody ID your ass," Patron said, sitting on the kitchen counter.

"Look, bruh, I saw the nigga with some redbone I knew. He owed, bruh, so I moved on him. The chick dropped him off. By the time he opened the door, I was on him with my nine," Gucci said.

"Ok, so what all happened? Don't leave a damn thing out," I said, knowing it was just another day in the life.

"Well, me and Pierre was cruising down Halstead Boulevard in E-City. So, I run into a thick bitch named Wanda I used to fuck with. Anyway, Wanda said Tyrone and some chic just dropped her off by the front of the Manor," Gucci Swagg said, trying to catch his breath.

"The Manor Housing Projects by the Handy Hugo store?" I said, knowing the housing area well.

"Yeah, well she say Tyrone been crashing at Trina house. That he be acting all nervous, and only ride with Trina. That's why we never saw that fool Chevy. But anyway, I know Trina. So, I tell Pierre I'd be right back. I walked to the back of the Manor, where I know Trina lived. I just caught her dropping the niggas off," Gucci Swagg said, sipping on a bottle of Avion Tequila. I realized for the first time his side was bleeding.

"Yo, nigga shot you?" I asked, glad he was ok.

"Yeah, he only grazed me though. That's what I was trying to tell Patron. The nigga got two bags from under her sink. My dumbass go to pick it up, that's when he pull on me. I fell back and shot the nigga. I grabbed the bags, but he still made it out the house. You know I couldn't let him live after that, Yay," Gucci Swagg said. I totally understood. Tyrone pulled first.

"I know, I know." I watched Patron roll a blunt. Pierre was leaning against the wall. "So, then what?"

"Once I got outside, I gave his ass a head shot. He was already hit in the back. I ran straight back to Pierre's truck," Gucci Swagg said.

"Fuck that!" Patron said, lighting the blunt. "The nigga dropped the damn gun."

"You fucking with me, right?" I said to Patron.

"Do I look like I'm fucking with you?" Patron said, staring at me.

"Did anybody see you? Anyone other than this Wanda chic?" I said to Gucci Swagg.

"Shit happened so fast, no one was really outside in the back of the Manor. By the time we peeled out, a few people came out, but we were gone," Gucci Swagg said, taking the blunt from Patron.

I walked over to the bags on the kitchen floor. I opened them up and in one bag was about thirty G's, give or take. The other bag had almost twelve grand and five ounces in it. Tyrone was acting like the shit was his. I counted out seven thousand dollars and let Pierre and Gucci Swagg split the work.

"You two split this shit down the middle. Pierre, I know you love that truck, but you got to get rid of it, ASAP. Don't know if anyone saw it," I said. Pierre took three pulls of the blunt, and damn near killed it.

"You see that shit? Now I know why your name Pierre Lunggington. Damn P-Funk," Patron said, rolling another blunt of sour diesel.

"I'm surprised I hit it, tight as you rolled it," he said, walking out the kitchen. "I'm going to handle that now, Yay," P-Funk said, leaving out to ditch the F-150.

"As for you, you got to sit your ass here until we hear anything. I appreciate what you did, homie, but remember…" I said, walking up to Gucci Swagg. "Never take your eyes off a scared nigga. Feel me?" I said seriously.

"Yeah, I got you, bruh." Gucci Swagg said, sitting on the couch. Patron had a fly cane I didn't notice because he had been sitting on the counter. Now that he was standing up, the cane was Louis Vuitton with the design all over the cane. Even matched his Louis Vuitton loafers. He limped towards me, then lit the newly rolled blunt with a Bob Marley Zippo lighter.

"What we going to do with these young hot heads, man? I tell you this, he better hope no one finds that gun. But at least we know they will pop our foes," Patron said, looking at Gucci Swagg with approval.

"Yeah, what can I say? I mean, Tyrone was MIA for over two weeks, even his phone was off. Gucci Swagg found him, got some dough and some work. We still got Larry Lawrence if shit go left," I said of the lawyer.

"Naw, after Han Che passed, that fool vanished. We got Bruce Smith. He's in the top five on the state," Patron said. It didn't dawn on me that I hadn't seen him since the funeral. I got a legal letter telling me my gun charge was dropped months after, but nothing else. I guess it must have affected Larry because he was, I'm sure, making a grip off Han Che in legal fees. I thought back to the funeral. I would have sworn he gestured me to call him, but we had left as soon as Han Che's casket was flown away. Well, once my charges was dropped, I never contacted Larry.

"Bruce Smith. Yes, I remember now. He like what, top ten in the state?" I said, remembering Shavonda with her lawsuit and her reminding me with my activities, I needed to keep a lawyer. Crazy, I didn't think about Larry until now.

"No homie, try top five in the state. If the system railroads you, next to Johnny Cochran, God rest his soul, you call Bruce." he said putting the blunt in the kitchen sink.

"Yo, Gucci Swagg, you sit tight. When we find out what's up, we will let you know. Until then, stay here, inside and out of sight," I said, walking out with Patron.

"I feel you, but what about a girl or something?" Gucci said turning the TV on, pouring himself a glass of Hennessy.

"Fool, you hot and on top of that, you dropped your strap. If you want to lay low somewhere else, be my guest. But don't make the cookhouse hot," I said.

"Technically, we don't cook shit, we sell the whole thing," Patron said, being sarcastic.

"Yo, Patron, shut the fuck up," I said, shaking my head. A nigga just caught a body and these fools got jokes.

Grinning, Gucci Swagg said, "Look. I got, you know, bitches. I'll stay put until you say different," Gucci Swagg said, watching *Set It Off* from the fifty-inch flat screen we had in the living room. It was only a two-bedroom apartment. I knew a girl that was about to get her own spot and didn't need it anymore. I paid her a nice amount and kept the paperwork updated by Milk Marie. But we had another chic doing it.

"Good, now let's take a ride, Patron," I said as we both went out the door. Patron knew me, so I didn't really have to say where we were going. We rode past the Manor Projects and there were police, yellow tape, and spectators everywhere. We kept driving and stopped at Tony's Pizza Parlor. I ordered a Heineken and large pizza with mozzarella. Patron ordered spaghetti. I loved Tony's because real Italians drank beer with their pizza, and at Tony's you could get smashed, as well as have a few slices.

"So, we just hope no gun was found and we keep Gucci Swagg at the cook spot. I'm telling you, Yay, we starting to recruit them too young," Patron said, shaking parmigiana cheese from a shaker onto his spaghetti.

"Shit, Pierre eighteen and Gucci Swagg only nineteen. I'm soon to turn twenty-five and you're twenty-four, Patron. We just more older minded than them. You can't say shit. You just had a guy chained to the wall in the basement," I said, eating two slices at once.

"Okay, but I didn't plan to kill him in broad daylight in the most rachet projects in the city," Patron said glancing at his watch.

I called Pierre to check on him, "I got a silver Chevy Silverado. It's still a truck, but definitely not an F-150. How Gucci doing?" Pierre said.

"He sitting still at the same spot you left him. Get whatever he needs. Tell him he is to only call you. No one else until we know what's up," I said.

"Say no more." P-Funk hung up.

"Yo, I need to make a move. You still riding with me or you going back to your car?" Patron said.

"I'm riding with you today, baller. I'm just trying to figure out why all hell broke loose. We haven't even been back that long after the shit in Spain," I said, paying the tip while Patron paid the check. He pushed the door open with his cane. Then he breathed in the fresh air outside.

"It's the life we live, Yay. I mean, shit, why don't we just retire? We got dough, so let's just bounce," Patron said, leaning on his Lexus.

"We still got a lot of shit going on. I want to move to Rio, but things just started to get good with El Jefe. Then, Shavonda wants to keep the house on the beach." As I was speaking, Patron was shaking his head from side to side, while putting out a Newport.

"You see," Patron said, lighting the cigarette. "It's all excuses, Yay. The truth is hustling is in our blood. We came from nothing, but it's like Money Making Mitch said to Ace in the movie *Paid in Full*, 'A nigga is like an NBA player. Yeah, we got dough, we can retire from the league, but will the fans still love us?'" Patron blew smoke out with a serious face. "I mean, shit, Han set you up just to get Han Che fucked up with the Russians. A year later, Han Che dead and we almost got smoked in Spain."

"So, what you saying, T.D. Jakes? You talking like you ready to go to church. I'm not going back to being normal. Fuck that. I'm not normal. I drive a two-hundred-thousand-dollar car, and my bitch look like Tisha Campbell, with a sprinkle of Amber Rose. Fuck else can I ask for?" I said, snatching the cigarette from Patron and throwing it away. I didn't smoke and I disliked any of my friends doing it. Patron walked up to me with a slight limp and held his cane up.

"You can ask for peace of mind. We legends in these streets. All I'm saying is I want to go out like Jordan did," Patron said, lighting another Newport.

"And how is that, homie?" I never heard Patron talk this way.

"I know other hustlers were before us and will be after us. But we did our things. Jordan jumped from the free throw line soaring through the air. Started calling him Air Jordan."

"It's other niggas that can do it now," I said.

"But not the way Jordan did it. He paved the way," Patron said, throwing the Newport down.

"Why you saying this now? Why you didn't stop?" I said, getting in the car. Patron got in and looked at me.

"Because we brothers and we get money over everything, fam," he said, dapping me up. "Broke niggas make noise."

"While rich niggas make moves," I said as we drove off.

Fre$h

Chapter 8

What Goes Up...

A few days went by after me and Patron had that talk. Shit, everything was good. No word about the incident Gucci Swagg got into. Even though we still kept him at the cook house, Pierre had some chics they had met in South Carolina on a run, link up with them at the apartment. I had bought an all-white Infiniti Coupe. I had a few runs to make in town, and I didn't want to draw attention to my Lambo.

I never smoked in any of my cars, but I had some new blue cheese loud I got from my white boy, Dee. He was from Durham, but he moved to E-City to help his uncle Tony, who owned Tony's pizza, out. But he had come from nine ounces and now was buying half a key. I tried to give him a whole key because I saw his hunger, but like me, he never did consignment. I liked that about him. He always had some good loud from Durham. Once I had a chance to pull over, I would roll one.

My eye caught my rearview mirror, and there was an unmarked car right behind me. *Shit!* I thought. I had half an ounce in my pocket, but I wasn't speeding so I kept cool. *I'm so glad I got my license situated.* I turned left off Bottom Avenue, but the car turned with me. I rode past the ballpark by the armory. That's when the car's red and blue lights flashed.

"Fuck," I said, while pulling over, calming myself. I was legit, but the police always mess with a brother in a nice car. I was truly glad I didn't drive the Lambo in town. Out stepped a black guy with salt and pepper hair, brown skin complexion with a medium build. Black shirt, gray pants, black shoes, and badge on his belt. I rolled down my window to greet the officer.

"Yes, sir, did I do something wrong?" I said.

"License and registration, young man. Nice car you have here," he said smiling, and I didn't like his demeanor. I gave him my license, registration, and started to dial for my lawyer. What he said next caught me off guard.

"No need to make any calls, Yay. I won't take much of your time," he said, looking around, giving my license and registration back. "This car is registered to a Shavonda P. Carter, age thirty. You, my friend, are Seemiyun Baxter, aka Yay," he said as if he just got a perfect score on his SATs. "Oh, my apologies. How rude. My name is Officer Dickerson, E-City PD."

"I don't know what this is about, but you must be misinformed, *Dick*," I said with anger. I hate fucking cops, but I know I had to be calm. I didn't have any handcuffs on, so I asked the obvious question. "What do you want?"

"What all of us want, Mr. Baxter. Money," he said, looking around. "Let's cut to the chase. I have a 9-millimeter with Rasheed Jacobs's fingerprints on it. Tyrone Dove is a homicide case. Word is, Rasheed is one of your boys, and a truck fled the scene. Unfortunately, no one can recall the color of the truck, but with the gun, it's a slam dunk." He adjusted his mirrored glasses.

"And if I refuse to deal with you?" I said, trying to hold in my anger.

Officer Dickerson took in a deep breath, and all of the politeness left his face. "Well then, I would have the feds breathing down your neck. You see, I'm not here to judge. Sell all the damn dope you want, but in E-City, you pay to play. You agree to my terms and we good."

"And the terms are?" I asked, staring at him, gritting my teeth until it hurt.

"For starters, ten K up front for the gun. Tyrone was a piece of shit anyway. He was going to turn state, but hey, what goes up must come down. Anyway, ten K every month, second Thursday. Every month. That's the terms and then I go my way, you go yours," he said, standing up from crouching while looking in the window.

"And how long do we do this dance, Officer Dick?" I said with attitude.

He pulled off his shades and stared at me. "When I say the music stops." Then he threw his card in my lap. Walking off, he yelled, "Two days. If my phone rings, I have your answer." Then just like that, turning his lights off, he was gone. This was a bad problem.

Even though I had not called Wang in a while, I knew he would take care of this. But everything comes with a price. "Yeah, Wang, it's me. Got a little issue. Yes, I need everything you got on an Officer Dickerson."

I was at Wang's mansion in less than an hour. We greeted each other and Fujj gave his signature grunt, then shut the big oak door to the study that used to be Han Che's.

"Yay, I looked this guy up. He is a nasty one. This Corey T. Dickerson been on the force for years. He started when he was twenty-seven years old. He is fifty-two. Wife by the name of Jessica Dickerson. Two boys, Todd and Tyler. Todd, nineteen, and Tyler, eighteen, both attend Belmont High near Tidewater," Wang said, chewing his Cuban cigar.

"Belmont, that's a private school. How the hell this dude afford that on a cop's salary?" I said, looking at Wang across the huge mahogany desk Han Che had loved.

"Really, Yay, you know damn well how he can afford it. Even has a cozy house in Belmont. Now, he has been under investigation twice actually. Nothing ever stuck. His wife's mother, Tiffany Swanson, passed away five years ago. So, the paper trail of their funds as a married couple was confirmed. Think the chief of police is in on it as well."

"Why you say that, Wang?" I said.

"Well, two years ago, a guy burned alive in his car. A witness claimed a guy fitting Dickerson's description opened the trunk of the car and fled from the scene with a duffel bag. The witness was a, um..." Wang said, scanning his laptop, "Wanda Mitchell was her name." Wang removed his reading glasses.

"So, what happened to this Wanda witness?" I said, finally rolling a blunt of blue cheese.

"She recanted her statement. Somehow, she couldn't be sure if it was a black or white male. So, she was deemed not credible."

"That son of a bitch got to her. That's cool though. I got a trick for his ass," I said to myself aloud.

"So, what you got in mind?" Wang said, all ears now.

"I'm going to play his game, for now anyway, but it's time to clean up, Wang. I'm tired of looking over my shoulder," I said, lighting the blunt.

"So, you've thought of my proposition then. Just assist Milk Marie with the DNA, and my paranoid mind will be clear. Trust me, Mr. Dickerson will not be an issue," Wang said, lighting his Cuban and leaning back in his chair.

"Yes, I've thought about it. I'll give you the details in a few days Wang. Do you have eyes on your mark? I mean, before we make this final, I need to know. You know everything for this to be a flawless situation," I said, inhaling the exotic smoke.

"This is what I do, Yay. I already have everything on go. Hell, I was ready weeks ago, but you had your doubts. I understand that, but it's past time. You know why me, as well as Fujj, joined Han Che's ranks."

Wang pushed a button on the desk, and the wall behind him moved. He stood up from the desk and buttoned up his three-piece Tom Ford suit. As he walked behind the desk, he looked at me and waved me over. "Come and see," Wang said.

I stood up, put my blunt out in the gold ashtray on the desk, and walked behind the desk to the hidden room. There was something gold in a big glass case. Wang wanted me closer, and as I came closer, I noticed it looked like a statue with no body. I think it was called a bust. As if Wang was reading my mind, "This, Yayo Sun, is not a bust. Please take a closer look," Wang said as he backed away.

I got closer and looked at the sculpture. It was the head of a Chinese person. The face had an expression of pain or shock. Then, I truly looked at it closely. "Holy shit, Wang! That's a real fucking head, man." I backed up a little "who head is that?" I asked. I already knew, but I had to hear Wang say it.

"It's the head of He. The one who killed Han Che's wife Charlotte. The cause of Han's anger, as well as wanting revenge for his mother's death," Wang said.

"Why didn't Han Che show this to Han? Let it be known he avenged Charlotte?" I said, staring at the head. The face of He looked dangerous in death. I could only imagine how He was in real life.

"Han's anger was too far gone. If Han Che allowed He access to the lifeline, it would have been chaos. He killed Charlotte for one reason and one reason only. She was in love with Han Che. The issue with the pipeline was just to start a feud. He knew Han Che would refuse, hell, He counted on it. Americans have their way, and we have ours. There was a private meeting between the cartel and Triad. Han Che brought He's head to the meeting. The feud ended and Fujj, as well as myself, joined Han Che. Han Che dipped He's head in gold and kept it as a reminder not to cross him," Wang said seriously.

"Well, whoever spiked his bottle didn't get the memo."

"That's why I'm here," he took his shades off, "because what goes up, Yayo Sun, must come down," Wang said, putting his shades back on, hiding his sacrifice for Han Che. I looked at the head once more before we left out the room. I took my original seat, and so did Wang. He pushed the button on the desk and the wall went back to normal.

"So, you still think Ken Chew could be Han?" I asked, relighting the other half of my blunt.

"Honestly, I have my doubts. But buying the property in Atlanta was a mistake. It raised a red flag for me. Even if I'm just paranoid, this Ken Chew is set up in Atlanta. Now all things considered, certain things are fair game. It's not like I hustle on a block, then you come on it and we have a feud," Wang said, pouring himself some whiskey. "The world is huge, Yayo Sun, with enough money for everyone. So, we have rules, structure, and things like that."

"Are you saying black people can't get along, Wang?" I said, feeling the blunt.

"First of all, you said that. I didn't. But since we are on the subject, look at the whites who have ruled with violence but stick together. The Indians even fought for their land. Koreans, as well as Chinese, have a piece of what is ours. I read a book called *BMF Rise and Fall of a Dynasty*. This Big Meech was intelligent, and he also had the right idea. But as Han Che would say, about being seen…"

"It's not the picture, but the flash of the camera that blinds you," I said, remembering.

"Right, Yayo Sun. Do you know why you stopped putting big rims on your car? Why you stopped wearing a lot of jewelry? Because you last longer, not allowing the flash of the camera to blind you." Wang said, downing the liquor. "Hardly anyone in this city even knows who Han Che was. This is why less is more. You understand?"

"Yes, I do, and I miss Han Che as well as his wisdom. We got to find who killed him," I said louder than I meant.

"And we will, Yayo Sun. I will have everything handled for you. I already have two of my best men out there in Atlanta. They will brief you on everything when you arrive." Wang stood up, which meant the meeting was over.

As he walked me to the door, he put his huge hand on my shoulder. "Thank you, Yayo Sun. We will rectify this wrong. It is the law of what we do. Because Yayo Sun, what does up must come down."

Fre$h

Chapter 9

In Due Time...

Milk Marie was taking a shower, upset that she and Paul could not get along. He was the GM of Peabody's, and he was the first to try to mend the main of being apart from Yay. The water sprayed over her long hair, which fell to her plump behind, as she soaped her breasts while imagining Yay's touch. She had a fling here and there, but Paul was the only constant. The attraction just wasn't there as it once was. She craved for Yay, and she hoped her betrayal of sleeping with Han could be cast aside. Milk Marie was determined to help Wang, if it meant getting closer to Yay. She'd dressed up that day when Wang sent for her to get a reaction out of Yay.

She turned the water off and stepped out of the shower in all her glory. True, Milk Marie had been around the block. She liked to fuck, who didn't? But one thing she knew was men. As she toweled herself dry, her Galaxy phone buzzed. She wrapped the towel around her form, thick for a white girl, her dark hair making her look exotic. She looked at the phone and smiled to herself. Milk Marie sent the text out that would flush out Ken Chew. She agreed to attend a get-together at Mason Fine Arts, which was rumored Ken Chew partly owned.

She never revealed where she lived. Her *Instagram*, as well as *Facebook*, of course had her pictures. But the apartment down the other end of the strip wasn't in her name, a habit she picked up from Yay. After the issue with Han, she was cautious. She was indeed terrified it was Han. Milk Marie felt using herself as bait to help Wang's paranoia was worth it, if it meant getting closer to Yay.

After live music, cocktails and mingling, there was a wine tasting extravaganza Ken Chew wanted her to attend. She replied, "Maybe," on the messenger app.

Milk Marie walked to the bedroom where Shameeka, a petite redbone, was laying in her bed. Last night, she and Paul argued. Paul had unloaded his credit cards, bought her gifts, but her heart remained with Yay. So, after Paul left, she called up Shameeka.

The waitress made crazy tips at the Peabody, and Milk Marie was supervisor over them. Paul was told from the higher-ups to give her the promotion. She was proud of herself. Shameeka always gave her *that* look certain girls give. And if Milk Marie was nothing else, she was a freak and had a fetish for females. But they had to be sexy, and Shameeka looked like Paula Patton. They felt each other up at work, and sometimes gave each other quick kisses between shifts.

Shameeka was just a distraction, and she even asked if Paul was with a threesome. But he gave her the third degree, asking if his dick wasn't enough. Yay was confident, and she liked he was just as freaky. Just the thought of it made her wet. She kissed Shameeka on the neck.

"What time is it, Milky?" Shameeka's used her pet name for Milk Marie.

"It's about ten am, but I have a long day. You have to go into the Peabody," Milk Marie said, looking at her Movado watch. Shameeka rolled over on Milk Marie, pulling the towel free.

"True, but not before I make you pop one time, Milky," Shameeka said, licking her breast, then down her belly button to her shaved pussy. "Mmm… Fresh out of the shower. I like that," Shameeka said between slurps.

"Mmm… Right there, Meeka, don't play. Lick right there. Yes…" Milk Marie said, while running her fingers through

Shameeka's curly hair. As she climaxed, she thought of Yay's body and his confident, cold smile. Yes, Shameeka was a distraction, but a very good one.

Once Shameeka finished making Milk Marie tremble one last time, she left for a walk. Shameeka knew it was just sex but flirting with Milk Marie was better than her boyfriend kicking her ass.

After Shameeka left, Milk Marie called Wang. "How are you doing, big guy?" Milk Marie said.

"I'm fine, Marie. How are you and little Malcolm?" Wang replied.

"Good, good. My mom has him, and my other kids are away at camp. But look, he bit the bet," she said, getting to the point.

"How long before you meet with him?" Wang asked gently.

"About four days at most. You still have your people in place?" Milk Marie said, not wanting to ever be alone with this Ken Chew character.

"No worried. I've had a twenty-four-hour watch on Mr. Chew, even before I spoke with Yay. Speaking of Yay, have you talked with him?" Wang said.

"Not in a few days. He may have an issue with us going on this mission together," Milk Marie said, a little worried.

"My dear, everyone has their own agenda. All I need is the DNA. What happens between you and Yay, is between you and Yay. I'll call you later with all the details. I suggest you get your luggage in order," Wang said with his commanding voice.

"But are you still going to—" Before Milk Marie could finish, Wang interrupted her.

"Yes, you will have fifteen grand just for doing this. That, my dear, is our business," Wang said.

"Damn, you really think it could be Han?" Milk Marie said obviously being he was offering up cash like that.

"Let's just say, I want to make sure. Then your quest is over, and I will proceed with my own plans. So, we are good," Wang retorted.

"Yeah, we good, but I'm going nowhere out of the line of sight if I can help it. This isn't just about me. Regardless of my moment of weakness, he crossed everyone, just to get to Han Che. I'm doing this for Yay," she said.

"Don't forget, fifteen grand, Ms. Marie," Wang said matter-of-factly.

"As you said, big guy, everyone has their own agenda," Milk Marie said.

"Well, you have but a few days to try to fulfill it. Good talking to you, Ms. Marie," Wang said.

"See you in four days, big guy," Milk Marie said, hanging up. Even though she never got a penny from Yay, she realized she was getting major money. Yay even dressed different. She'd kicked herself once she came out Wang's mansion.

She slipped on her Paul Smith mini. It cost Paul fourteen hundred, to be exact. She was going to pick up Malcolm, hoping to see Yay later in the day. It hurt her to know the only reason she was alive was because of Malcolm.

Of course, she had seen this Shavonda girl a time or two, in her cherry red BMW around the beach. The girl was quite attractive, Milk Marie noted, but she and Yay still had a deeper bond. They had made a life together, and Milk Marie hoped it would be enough.

She walked out of her apartment with her burgundy Birkin bag matching her mini, finishing off the look with open-toed Jimmy Choo stilettos. There was no denying Milk Marie made heads turn, but no matter how she tried, the fact of being a jump-off was the harsh truth. She got in her Tahoe with Hello

Kitty car mats and stickers on the dashboard. She had it painted pink, and it fit her. In due time, she said to herself, Yay could forgive and forget. Sometimes she didn't like herself, but Yay had accepted her, flaws and all... She failed to be more than his baby mama. That would change if she had her way. Her phone rang, playing a Nicki Minaj song for her ringtone, "I beez in the trap, beez beez in the trap."

"Hello," she said, sliding her shades on.

"Hi, Shayla, and how are you these days?" Larry Lawrence said.

"Larry. Hi. Um, wow, where have you been? It's been rough the past few months," Milk Marie said. Larry was, at one time, a representative of the cartel. But no one had seen him since the funeral. Milk Marie last saw him when she got pulled over for a DUI, back when things were rocky with her and Yay.

"I was actually back on business. I had to take a break from Moyock, as well as the whole E-City scene," Larry said, "Anyway I wanted to talk to you about Han Che."

"Oh, well what about Han Che? Do you know who poisoned him?" Milk Marie asked, faster than Larry could even answer.

"Whoa, Whoa, Whoa... First of all, slow down. I can see we don't need to say anything else over the phone. I'll just get up with you when you're free, but don't tell anyone I called. I don't need that attention just yet," Larry said.

"That's cool, because Yay isn't exactly talking to me. But I'm going on a little vacation. So, I'll just hit you up." Milk Marie said, "But do you know anything?"

"I'll tell you what, when you get back, we can talk. I actually have to run. Until then, Shayla." Then Larry hung up.

Milk Marie put the pink lip gloss on her lips and put her Tahoe in drive. Now she felt Yay might listen to her. Larry had called, and he called her. He knew something. She could feel it. For now, she would keep it to herself. As she pulled out on the strip, the air had a chill, but the sun was shining brightly. As she turned Lil Weezy up on the radio, her phone buzzed. As *Tha Carter V* banged through the speakers, she took her phone from the middle console. It was Yay, and he said, "See little man for a few tonight?" Milk Marie looked back up at the road as she was driving. *Everything was coming along. Everything will come to the light in due time.*

Chapter 10

Lamborghini Mercy...

I was doing like a hundred and twenty in my Lambo. Patron was in the passenger seat, holding on for dear life. I had a guy who got three keys from me. He was the commissioner over a racetrack in Richmond. Everyone handles stress different. Some exercise. Some get high. But me, RIP Paul Walker, mine was speed.

I had been dogging the Lambo like Jay-Z and Kanye did when they chopped the top off the Maybach. I was doing donuts, even in reverse. After about thirty minutes, I chilled out, pumping *Tha Carter V* in my radio loud. "Money on my mind, Money on my mind, Money on my mind, Money is all I think of." Patron turned down the radio staring at me.

"Yo Yay, next time you got anger issues, do me a favor, don't pick me up. Nigga, you been doing donuts, three-sixties, and damn near flipped us. What's good? Holla at me, because the heart attack I can do without."

I lifted the doors open while drinking a bottle of Evian water. I was leaning against the car. I took a deep breath and confided in my boy.

"So, I go to see Wang, right? You know, to get me some info on this Dickerson clown that's shaking me down. And bruh, fuckin Wang shows me the head of the guy that killed Han's mom," I said, still seeing his face in my mind.

"Holy shit, a human head? So, Wang and Fujj are like fuckin Jeffrey Dahmer, man? Why the fuck would they be keeping a head?" Patron said, taking a swig of Hennessy out the bag.

"Not just keeping it, but they got the damn thing dipped in twenty-four-karat gold, Patron. I'm telling you I'm glad they on our side," I said, rolling a Garcia Vega of some sour diesel.

"That's some movie shit," Patron said, taking another sip.

"No, fool, that's some real shit. I saw it. Whoever this Ken Chew fool is got problems. So, you going out tonight or what?" I asked, finishing rolling my morning fix.

"Naw. Lisa got my dick in her pocket. We chillin tonight, watching *Netflix*. I got Pierre handling something for me so I could chill with Lisa," Patron said, getting back in the car. I got back in as well. Patron looked at me, shaking his head. "Only you would drive a two-hundred-thousand-dollar car like it's a damn dune buggy."

"Sorry, I got a lot on my plate. I gave that prick ten grand for Gucci Swagg's gun. I wanted to put a hole in his face so bad."

"So, Gucci Swagg know it's his, right?" Patron asked.

"Yeah, he took it apart right in front of me. Said his uncle taught him how to do it. Right after he taught him how to steal cars. Anyway, his time's coming. I get to see little Malcolm tonight anyway," I said on our way back to Virginia Beach.

"That's what's up. So look, just go to Atlanta, feel me? Handle that thing-thing and then when you get back, I'll wrap up everything. You say Wang got two guys already up there," Patron said, passing me the Hennessy. I looked at him like he was crazy.

"You know what Young Jeezy said, fool?" I told Patron, but he had already stolen my line.

"Yeah, yeah, my partner on brown, but you know I'm on white. I know the damn song."

"Look, I met this bad ass exotic chic, bruh. I mean, Taylor Swift with a little Lady Gaga, I'm telling you. She had a cute

Givenchy dress on when I was at Starbucks," I said, surprised at how energetic I sounded.

"Hold up. I think I remember her at Han Che's funeral. Wavy brunette-like hair, but she's like British or some shit," Patron said, looking at his phone.

"Yes. She is from England and how do you remember her?" I said, because I didn't remember seeing her at the funeral.

"How do you know she is from England?" Patron said playfully.

"Stop asking a question with a question," I said frustrated.

"Damn, Tupac, cool out. I like that sushi shit, and they had some. I heard her talking to Wang and her voice sounded foreign. Plus, she looks like Emma Stone with a big booty and grey eyes," he said.

I did remember her eyes and her laugh was enchanting. I couldn't help but to hope I would bump into her again. I wonder how the hell she knows Han Che," I said, steering the car.

"I mean, you've seen her. She probably has perfume called Benjamins. Might be old money, but you can tell she is well off. Shit, maybe Han Che was hitting it, but all I know she got a mean body. What, you thinking about getting on yuh TLC shit?" Patron said laughing.

It's crazy. I never thought of another chic. I mean, I had my share before and after Milk Marie. Shavonda was my baby, so I shook it off. But I couldn't front, with that body and accent, she was in my head.

"Naw, look, as a matter of fact about to drop you off and go scoop my lady," I said, trying to dismiss his insinuations with Vicky.

"Whatever. If you hit it, you better tell me because I'm your boy," Patron said, finishing off the Hennessy. I was about to say something smart when my phone rang. It was Milk Marie.

"You busy, big time, or you got time to see Malcolm?" Milk Marie said with a snotty attitude.

"Damn. How you doing, Yay? I'm fine. What's up, Milk? Oh, nothing much. Why can't our conversations ever start like that?" I said, looking at Patron, who was making dumb faces, asking me who it was. I told him, and he started acting stupid. The sour diesel was kicking in.

"Yay, don't start, and what are you snickering about?" Milk Marie said.

Damn, Patron was singing TLC's song. "Yeah, I creep, yeah, just keep it on the down low." I kept shushing him while talking to Milk Marie, who seemed to be getting irritated.

"Yay, I thought you were coming to see your son. Are you coming or not?" Milk Marie said. I always, no matter what, kept my word.

"You know what, since you got an attitude, I'll be over in a few. It's apartment 31, right, on the fifth floor?" I said, knowing, but I had never been to her apartment.

"Yes, I didn't think you'd remember. Well, in that case hurry up. I got your favorite on ice," she said, sounding nicer.

"Oh, yeah? What's that?"

"I got a big bottle of Grey Goose. After work, it just happened to be in my possession. Plus, Malcolm a little rowdy today. Maybe once he sees Daddy, he may cool out."

"Goose, huh? Yeah, I'll be about twenty minutes then," I said, still cracking up at Patron singing.

"No doubt. I'll be waiting," Milk Marie said, hanging up.

"Yo, Patron, you a certified cornball. I'm going to see my kid," I said, noticing the way Milk Marie had said, "I'll be waiting."

"Man, you are turning twenty-four in another month. You got one kid," Patron said smiling, "that we know of." Then he said, looking around the interior of my car, "Damn shit got Gucci seats, Yay. These hoes going to fuck, bruh."

Once I pulled up to his six-room, five-bathroom, as well as a six-car garage in Emerald Isle Estates, I had to adjust. We were holding it down, but the dirty cop was bothering me. It was something familiar about him. I shook off the thought as Paton stumbled out of the car.

"Whoa, homeboy, don't let Lisa catch you like that. You good?" I said, looking out the passenger side while the doors were still up.

Patron straightened his stand a little and said, "I'm good once I get a Red Bull in, I'll mellow out. I know you love Shavonda, but Victoria got you cheesing, bruh. For real though. And be careful in Atlanta. Now, if you'll excuse me." Patron brushed off his shoulder with his Louis Vuitton cane in his hand. "I got to sober up for *Netflix*." We both started laughing. I knew Lisa was understanding of this life, and she loved Patron.

I was pushing it a little, and I slowed down once I got to Volvo Parkway. On my way to the strip, I kept wondering why Officer Dickerson looked familiar. Shit kept bugging at me like a fly on a summer day around a picnic. Once at the strip, I went to go pay my parking fee. Shavonda and I lived on the other end of the strip, more near the Peabody restaurant.

The Dynasty Apartments were at the end of the carnival, and you will pass a million 7-Eleven's in Virginia. I stopped at one across from Dynasty Apartments. I wolfed down two hot dogs on the way up to Milk Marie's apartment. I was pretty much chilling today. I had on denim Levi's. All-black shirt, with the picture of my mother swinging from the Figaro chain to my stomach, and some comfortable Steve Madden sneakers on. As I approached the elevator, I was making sure I had no mustard on me. After getting off the elevator, I noticed the door was slightly open. As I got closer, I heard arguing.

"Paul, you need to cool off. Either you're drunk or you just lost your mind. My son's father will be here soon," Milk Marie said angrily.

"So, is that who you're fucking? Is that why we only fuck if I'm buying you something? I was there when you were pregnant, and we work together." Paul said, upset, "I thought you wanted this to work."

"Look, I'm confused and I have a lot going on. But you raising your voice in here with my son. You better chill," Milk Marie said, opening the bedroom door, peeking in on little Malcolm.

"Fuck that! I deserve an explanation. And why are you going on a trip in a few days? What is that shit about?" Paul said, again too loud.

"For one, I'm grown and for two, I went through Laura for my vacation time. So, how did you know anything about it?" Milk Marie said, now agitated that Paul was all in her business.

"I'm still the GM, and you going through Laura lets me know you didn't want me to know," Paul said, walking up in Milk Marie's face.

She closed the door and politely said, "Look, let's talk about this later, okay? You're drunk, Paul, and my son is resting," Milk Marie said, hoping the tone of her voice would get him to leave. Paul was all up on her now.

"Okay. Well, let me get sum right quick. I miss hitting that, baby," Paul said, trying to feel her ass.

"Fool, did you just hear me? My son is asleep in the other room. Paul, stop," Milk Marie said when Paul tried to kiss on her.

I'd had enough of what I was hearing, so I walked in. "Knock, Knock. Yo, Milk, what's up?" I said, walking in the middle of her spacious living room. She never asked me for money, but I took care of Malcolm regardless. It was a nice apartment, but this wasn't the time to compliment her on it. "Oh, you have company. My bad," I said, trying to stay cool. Paul was the kind of guy a girl could meet. The kind that didn't like the word no. He was backing up from Milk Marie a little.

"Oh, um... no, no he was just leaving. Isn't that right, Paul?" Milk Marie looked a bit nervous but pissed to be caught in such an awkward situation. Paul somehow got his nerve back.

"Yes, I was just leaving." Then he looked at Milk Marie. "But we will talk later," he said, walking towards the door. My adrenaline was pumping. I let my rage take over.

"Let me walk you to the door, homie." I said, walking by the door and as soon as he came close enough, I pulled my Desert Eagle out. *BAM, BAM* I smacked him over the head twice. Then I put my gun back in my waistband and gave him three powerful overhead rights to the face. *Pop, Pop, Pop* He sunk to the floor, and I squatted down to him. I slapped him in the face several times. "Hey! Hey, wake up!"

Once his eyes fluttered open, he looked as if he didn't know how he got on the floor. When I had his attention, I politely said to him, "I don't care what you have going on with Milk Marie, but I just gave you a small lesson. If you ever disrespect her in my presence, I will kill you. If you conduct yourself like this around my son, I will kill you. If any issue comes up at her job because of this issue, I'll kill you. Do you understand?" I said, dreads hanging down in front of my face, eyes looking like slits. I was so angry. He didn't respond. So, I took out my gun and cocked it. "Do you understand?"

All of a sudden, Paul nodded his head at me, shaking. "Now, get the fuck out of here," I said, standing to my full height of six-three, as Paul struggled to get up. Once he was out the door, Milk Marie just stared at me. I wasn't going to give her a lecture on the dirt bags she dealt with. I wasn't the one for that. I just wanted to see Malcolm.

"Oh, my God! Yay, your hand. Your knuckles are bleeding," Milk Marie said, looking around her kitchen. I noticed the big bottle of Grey Goose in a bucket of ice on her dining room table. I grabbed the bottle with my left hand and sat in a chair, sticking my right hand in the ice bucket.

"Oh, that's nice. Um, Milk, can you pop the top on this?" I said, wincing a little with my hand in the ice.

She popped the cork and poured herself a drink, then poured one for me also. I still reached for the bottle and took a swig. Milk Marie shook her head and said, "I knew you were going to do that. You got expensive taste, but still drink out the bottle," she said laughing.

"Well, you know what they say. You can take the nigga out the hood, but not the hood out the nigga. By the way, this spot nice," I said, looking around. It was well furnished and very clean.

"Yeah, I work hard. The kids come over at times, but once I save up, I'll be good. Here, let me," she said, wiping my right hand off with a towel, then wrapping a small Ace bandage around my knuckles. "There you go, Mike Tyson." She walked past me. The Paul Smith mini looked sexy as hell on her, and she was barefoot, showing off her pretty toes on her wooden floor. I took another drink off the bottle and went to see my son. As I opened the door, I heard the loud sounds of

Sade singing. I walked up to the bed, and he was sound asleep in a baby Trukfit jumper.

"I love you, little man. You rest now." I kissed his forehead. With Milk Marie behind me, we tiptoed out the door.

"He is getting big for real. Yo what's up with the Sade music?" I said, going back for the bottle.

"Excuse me, like father like son. When he starts acting up, I put some Sade on and he good after ten minutes. I know everyone hear you playing Jay-Z, Tupac, or Two Chainz everywhere you go. But I," Milk Marie said, walking circles around my chair, "know you love Sade, Erika Boykin, and especially Mary J Blige." She pulled a chair up and kicked her foot on my lap.

"Well, I used to always hear my aunt play it when I lived with her a few years. But what's up with the lame you had up in here, Milk?" I said, feeling the Goose. Then I looked up her leg to her mini. She had no panties on.

"Paul is mad because it's just not what I thought it was. Like, some dude was hitting on me and another girl. Now, all I do is get you to your table, if no other waitresses are available. Well now every time that guy comes, he sits him in the back. I don't like jealous dudes. Shit is real corny. Anyway, I haven't been dealing with him in a while, now he sour," she said, rubbing my crotch with her feet. "I know you meant well, but Paul looks pretty bad."

"Fuck Paul, he lucky that's all I did. In here like that with my son" I said, taking another sip of the Goose, sitting it back on the table. I was feeling good. I sat back, ran my fingers through my long locks. Milk Marie moaning and biting her lips while looking at me had my attention. I felt I was moving in slow motion.

"I used to love watching you push those dreadlocks out your face. Mmm, mmm, shit sexy," she said, lifting her mini skirt then playing in her pussy, staring at me.

The liquor had me, and Milk Marie's hair was falling over one eye down her right side. I was sitting at an angle to her left. She was licking her lips, gently massaging her clitoris.

I tried to speak up, mouth dry, my manhood was bursting through my jeans. My words slurred a little as I finally spoke. "They are locks, not dreads, because the British and other different nationalities said they were dreadful. So therefore, I only call them locks," I said, feeling way too tipsy.

She then walked up to me and unzipped my pants. Making a noise of approval, she pulled my dick free from my jeans. As she slowly stroked it, I was in a pleasurable trance. Milk Marie knew me, knew my body, and its likes. I tried to resist but her hands felt so good. As she stroked me, she spoke gently in a very special way. Giggling, she said, "Remember when we first met and right before I would taste you, you always asked me, 'Why do they call you Milk Marie?'" she said, squatting to lick the tip, then she took all of me in her mouth. It was so hot, and she did this thing where she beat it against her tongue. Then she straddled me, and I knew I'd lost the battle. Her long hair fell down her back. I gripped her ass and had handfuls of her hair.

"That's it, baby. Squeeze my ass! Fuck, I missed this dick, Yay."

We were just forehead to forehead, bucking until waves of orgasm took her. I tried to get a bit of my senses under control and pull out, but she kept licking my neck, her ass slamming on my waist. Once I came, it was several violent jerks. Before I knew it, I had her in midair. Once the lust passed, I felt a wave of guilt take me over. I pulled my pants up, went to the sink and splashed water on my face. I was pissed I had betrayed Shavonda, but what pissed me off more was, I had enjoyed every minute of it. I turned, toweling my face.

"Look, Milk, ummm…" I started to say, but she interrupted me.

"Yay, I love you. Okay? We fucked, so just don't trip. I'm not that kind of baby mama. I know I hurt you, regardless of how our arrangement was." But then she walked up to me with the smell of my manhood on her breath. "But I don't regret tonight. Lord knows I needed that," Milk Marie said, looking me up and down like a steak.

"We have a son, and I have a lot on my mind. I'll see myself out," I said, walking towards the door. As I got to the door and opened it to leave, Milk Marie got all in my face.

"You can hate me, and you can think what you want. But know this, Seemiyun Baxter, she cannot fuck or suck you like me," Milk Marie said, puckering her lips up for a kiss. I just looked at her, seeing all the memories of her doing God knows what, back when I wanted more. I walked right past her out the door.

"Later, Milk. See you in Atlanta in a few days," I said, leaving.

"Fuck you, Yay. Fuck you!" Milk Marie yelled down the hallway. I didn't respond at all. I felt like shit, and I had to make a note never to drink around Milk Marie again.

My phone had seven missed calls. Every last one of them was from Shavonda, and a few texts too. I was heated because if it wasn't for Wang's paranoid notion, I would have never been around Milk Marie. After Atlanta, I was taking my ass to Rio, because I was definitely reminded of why her name was Milk Marie.

Fre$h

Chapter 11

Another Day, Another Dollar...

Luckily, the walk home sobered me up. Once I got home, Shavonda was knocked out sleep. I took a quick shower, put my Gucci pajamas on, and slid into bed. Once the warmth from Shavonda's ass was up against me, I felt even more dumb, but right now I was exhausted. Shavonda wrapped her legs around mine, which was her thing. I loved that, and then I dozed off. I dreamed I was in nothing but darkness, and then I heard Han Che's voice. "Yayo Sun, all enemies must be exterminated. This is the balance that has to be kept." Then a light glowed, and He's head was glowing in gold. Then Han Che's voice whispered again, "An example must be set. They are not who they say they are."

Then I smelled coffee, and I began to wake up. Prince was playing in the living room. "This is what it sounds like when doves cry." I knew she was in some kind of mood.

I got up, brushed my teeth, and washed my face. Then I put on some Hugo pants and a Dolce & Gabbana shirt. Then I slipped on my Dolce & Gabbana loafers, along with a little Prada cologne she had bought me. I wanted to be relaxed today and my attire, though designer, was quite comfortable. I had a special made .380 tucked in a leather waist holder. I had been shot, and I vowed to never be without a gun ever again.

As usual, Shavonda was in the kitchen. She had toast on plates with butter and jelly on several pieces of toast. She handed me a plate. I took it as I looked at her curves. Shavonda was indeed sexy. Her hair was blonde, with finger waves going down the left side of her face, and with her redbone complexion, she looked a little like Blac Chyna. She had on a denim Versace jean outfit with a Versace sports bra with the jacket open. The word Versace was in white letters all over the denim outfit. It fit her curves perfectly.

"When you get that outfit? That shit fly," I said, pouring myself a mug of coffee.

"Justin Bieber is dating Hailey Baldwin, and I saw it in a magazine. I wanted to switch it up, you know how I do," she said, nibbling on toast. I knew something was bothering her, so I left her alone and waited for her to tell me.

"Baby, you want to just get out of here today? You know, just me and you," I said, walking up to her.

She walked up closer to me and said, "I would love that Yay," pouring her leftover coffee in the sink. So, we took her BMW. I liked her model because the top came down. And it was a nice day. The air was crisp, and it would be chilly later for sure.

We went to the carnival, and I won her a big teddy bear. We rode a few rides and even got on the Ferris wheel, which Shavonda was truly terrified of. But today, she rode with me, and for a while I forgot about last night. I loved Shavonda, and I knew I wouldn't let it happen again. But I knew she was still financially able to hold herself down. She loved me for me, and shit like that was rare. I had been through the *Facebook* chicks lying, with three or four baby daddies, or *Instagram* chicks that looked nothing like their photos. No, Shavonda was the real thing. It turned me on that she was older.

We had a great day, and I never touched my phone. Something I know she noticed and appreciated. It wasn't that late when we got home. Shavonda tore my clothes off. I loved it when the smell of the Prada drove her crazy. I thought I was trapped in an Axe commercial as she snatched at my Hugo pants. I had already kicked off my Dolce & Gabbana loafers. We fucked right in the living room, then I had her bent over the counter in the kitchen. Once we got to the bedroom, she was looking up at me while were in the missionary position. We climaxed at the same time, and a tear ran down her face. She then rubbed my face gently, and then out of nowhere, smacked the shit out of me.

"Shavonda, what the fuck, ma?" I said, looking down at her.

"Let's get one thing straight, Yay. I love you, and I'm down, boo. Trust me. Whatever the fuck you did, I forgive you. Just promise me the shit won't happen again," she said, looking into my eyes with her damn near emerald-green irises looking through me. "Whatever that issue may be." I got up to let her up, and she walked out of the bedroom. I never responded, but the whole time she knew. I threw some jogging pants on and sat at the foot of the bed. I lit up a blunt of purple. Shavonda peeked her head in the bedroom.

"Hey, boo, will you watch *Half Baked* with me?" Shavonda said in a girly voice. And like that, all was forgiven. I got up and passed her the blunt.

"Yeah, boo, we can watch it. You think you bad, slapping me and shit?" I said, slapping her big ass.

"Shoulda brought your ass home, not two am drunk. Got me worried," she said, shaking her big booty. Damn, I was truly lucky and thankful we were past that. Shavonda was like that. Once she said something, that was it. I had to get my head back in the game. Chicks love to catch niggas slipping and like it or not, Milk Marie was that kind of chick. The kind that fucks you to sleep and goes through your pockets, while you napping off that good loving. Shavonda was quite the opposite. My phone started ringing, interrupting my thoughts.

"What's good, partnuh, speak to me? Kind of late, isn't it?" I said to Patron.

"No shit. I been hitting your cell all day. You need to hit up Wang pronto," Patron said.

"Damn, playa, where's the fire? I thought I wasn't supposed to deal with Atlanta for at least three more days," I said watching Shavonda load the DVD player with one of her favorite movies.

"Well, you would be up to speed if you picked up your phone. What's up, Yay? You always answer your shit," Patron said, prodding me.

"Just wanted to spend some quality time with Shavonda. So, we went out, and I just didn't want to be on my phone like I usually do," I said.

"Now, that's bullshit. Something smells." Then the line got quiet. Patron remembered. "I was drunk and you were going to see lil Malcolm. Oh shit, Yay, you boned Milk Marie, didn't you?" Patron said laughing.

"Fuck you for one, and for two, let's get to why you calling me so late. So, what's up? I said, changing the subject.

"I know you hit it. I told you either her or that Victoria chic that look like fuckin Sharon Stone were going to get you. Anyway, when you were on your date, apparently Ken Chew did a brief pop-up on Milk Marie at the Peabody. Claims he was coming from Maine on business and stopped briefly on the strip in the restaurant to speak."

"Shit, this happen today, or should I say tonight?" I said.

"Yeah, about two hours ago, and Wang wants to speed up dangling Milk Marie for bait," Patron said.

"When exactly is that?" I asked.

"You'll be leaving tomorrow, but as I said, Wang will fill you in. He has already briefed Milk Marie, and I only know what I know because no one could get ahold of you. So, I was to pass it on if I got up with you first," Patron said.

Then my phone beeped. "Speak of the devil. It's Wang. I'll hit you back," I said.

"Broke niggas make noise," Patron said.

"Rich niggas make moves," I said, clicking over to talk to Wang. "It's getting late," I said, hoping to keep it short. Shavonda was rolling her eyes at me with *Half Baked* playing on our seventy-inch flat screen.

"Ahh, my apologies, Yayo Sun, but I need you to take the trip a bit early. I already have everything arranged. Milk Marie is already on her way to Atlanta. She seemed to have an attitude, but more cooperative to the time with Ken Chew," Wang said.

"If she wants to throw a tantrum and put herself in that situation, that's on her. Regardless of how I may feel, she betrayed me," I said irritated. My guilt was coming back. I glanced at Shavonda and lowered my voice. "I'll call tomorrow. What time is my flight?" I asked.

"Around lunch, so eleven am, be ready to roll. I have my two best assassins, Ying and Yang, already based in Atlanta. They will also grab Milk Marie when she gets there," Wang said with authority.

"And are these the mole or moles in the Triad you spoke of?" I asked.

"No, not exactly. They assisted Han Che some years back when they were very young. They have been killing since they were ten years old. The first mission is how they are in our ranks now. They will be of good use. They have been on full surveillance of Ken Chew's movements for months now. He's popping up in Virginia to so-call "see" Milk Marie. Has me more anxious to get his DNA," Wang said.

"And then?" I said.

"And then we wait for the results, but I don't like this guy. Everything about him feels wrong," Wang said.

"Wrong how, Wang? It's all got to be more than just a gut feeling, old friend," I said, seeing Shavonda's impatience. I held up one finger to her.

"Okay, remember the property that got purchased around Han Che's funeral?" Wang said.

"Yeah, you said that's what sent up a red flag for you in the first place," I said, remembering.

"Right, well in Milton, Georgia, is one of the locations where we own our whiskey business. Not only that, but every year we have a whiskey festival in Milton as well. We own the property the festival is on and let me tell you, it's legendary. We even had Willie Nelson perform there. Huge, huge event, as well as profit margins for the cartel," Wang said, trying to get me to understand.

"Okay, so if it's huge and does well, what's the issue?" I said.

"The issue is we have the land, but the landowner, whose name is on the deed, was made a hell of an offer by an anonymous buyer," Wang said it as though to say to me, "TADA."

"So, you think it's Ken Chew? The anonymous buyer?" I said.

"Who else would it be, and it's another one of our properties. If the person we had was not loyal to the cartel, that unnamed would own it. Yayo Sun, in business you don't need a name. Not when you have numbers. Big six-figure numbers at that. So, kill an old fool's curiosity and we will be done with this," Wang said.

"Okay. See you tomorrow, Wang," I said.

"Tomorrow indeed, Yayo Sun." He hung up.

I jumped on the couch and kissed Shavonda and took the freshly rolled blunt from her hand. We smoked and giggled at David Chapelle's genius stoner movie. I tried not to think of Milk Marie just leaving like that, but all of that could wait until tomorrow. I pushed Shavonda back on the couch and started kissing her stomach. She started to moan. "So much for the movie," she said as my tongue danced around her clitoris. We made love all night. Once we were out of breath for the third time, she said, "So, where are you going, Yay?" as her chest rose and fell rapidly.

"Why you say that?" I said, leaning up on the pillows of the huge couch.

"Boy, you only sex me like that when your ass is going somewhere," she said, pillowing the blanket I'd brought from the closet.

"Atlanta. I have business in Atlanta I have to attend to, but it won't be long, baby. No more than a day or two."

"Well, I have a big clearance sale at the shop. I have to make room for my supplies I have coming in. Thank you for the idea with the towels. Princess did a survey of people that came in to buy them. It was two hundred and fifty people, so the math should hold up," she said, leaning back on the couch pillows.

"I told you, baby. Every time I've ever gone to the beach at the spur of the moment, I damn near always leave my towel. Trust me, sales will go up," I said confidently, rubbing her feet.

"That's why you the hustler. Yay, baby?" Shavonda said, looking in my eyes.

"Yeah, baby, what's up?" I said, rubbing her feet and making her giggle.

"I'm serious, Yay. Stop, boo," she said smirking.

"Okay, okay. What's up? Holla atcha boy," I said, loving when we were like this. Just us being us.

"Promise me you will get out of this life. I know about you wanting to go to Rio. Shit, you damn near talk about it in your sleep," she said smiling.

"Yeah. I don't talk about it much because I don't want to jinx it. Either Rio or Italy. Honestly, Italy wouldn't be bad."

"Well, either way, I don't want this life to pull us apart. I love you, Yay," she said, curling up beside me on the couch.

"I love you too and as soon as I come back, we going to Italy. We can talk about retirement there," I said smiling.

"It's a date, baby," Shavonda said as we fell asleep.

Chapter 12

Going To See the Wizard...

I woke up on the couch, smelling like Tom Ford Eau du Soleil Blanc for women, and sex. Shavonda left a note for me to have a safe trip, and she had to get the clearance section of her shop finished, as well as order the towels. I jumped in the shower while the house stereo blasted "OOOUUU," Young M.A.'s hot song. "You can call her Stephanie, we call her Headphanie." Once out of the shower, I put on some wheat Timbs, Levi jeans, black shirt, chain with my mom's picture, Gucci shades, and my dreads in a ponytail falling down my back. I had two Gucci suitcases. I was on my way to catch the plane, while Wang was talking to me through my Bluetooth earpiece.

Once I got there, Ying and Yang were going to brief me. Ken Chew was going to host an event in downtown Atlanta. All we were supposed to do, honestly, was babysit Milk Marie. Ying and Yang didn't know Milk Marie. Whether they were going to end up doing the hit was not told to me. I was supposed to keep an eye on Milk Marie.

She would use this device that looked like a gold bracelet, but when it was removed it could be made to straighten out. You pressed a button and a small needle poked out. The plan was for her to find an opportune time to poke Ken Chew, get his DNA, and then jet. Once the twins, Ying and Yang, got the DNA we could leave. We were only here because Ken Chew obviously had an interest in Milk Marie. For whatever reason, Wang was in a hurry.

I boarded the plane with so much on my mind, listening to Bryson Tiller in the iPod I carried. Bryson's voice was singing "Don't," in my ears. I could tell Wang was starting to have his doubts it was Han. This Ken Chew dude was just a thorn in Wang's side, businesswise, nothing more. I saw the writing on the wall. Being that I used to deal with Milk, I was around so she wouldn't feel alone. Besides, I had never met Ying nor Yang, but I had heard about them. I relaxed for the flight. I just hoped this would be over with soon. Something still bothered me about the cop I was paying off. Well, that would be dealt with once I got back. A flight attendant asked me what I was drinking. I got Grey Goose, no ice, wondering if Milk Marie's leaving early had to do with the other night.

Meanwhile in Woodbridge, Virginia...

Nancy Baxter lived alone, especially after her husband passed. Not too long after, she found out about Yay living with his foster parents.

The house was very nice and spacious in a gated community. Even though Nancy Baxter received money from her husband's death, because he was a veteran, the home still was a bit much more than Social Security could cover. She had two Great Danes that Yay had bought to protect her. The ringing doorbell startled her, because she was pouring herself some tea. She was about to watch *Love & Hip Hop Atlanta*, her favorite show. Back in her day, a man just paying the bills was a big deal. These girls were raking in money off celebrity guys. She often felt younger watching it.

As she approached the door, the dogs started growling low in their throats. "Marvin and Luther, behave," she ordered. Nancy named the dogs after her two favorite singers, Marvin Gaye and Luther Vandross. "Yes, who is it?" she said, irritated, ready to get back to her program.

"Police, ma'am, just like to ask you a few questions."

"A few questions about what? I know my rights," Nancy said, yanking the big oak door open. She was beyond shocked when it was Officer Dickerson at her door.

"How you doing, Nancy?" Then he looked around the house. The Great Danes growled but stayed where they were.

"You slimy bastard. You have some nerve showing up at my doorstep," Nancy said with the door still half-open.

"And at the looks of things, doing quite well. I have to talk to you about your nephew," he said, inching closer to the door.

The dogs barked loudly now. If he as much as touched Nancy, they would attack him. He backed towards the porch, understanding the warning of the dogs loud and clear.

"I have nothing to say to you and if you ever come back again, I'll call the real damn police," Nancy said with obvious anger.

"Tell him to stay away from Ken Chew. There is a lot at stake he doesn't know. Just let him know. You and your puppies have a good night," he said, walking down the steps of the house with a ten-acre lawn.

"Why don't you come pet them, you damn pig," she taunted as he drove away. She sat down and put her feet up in her recliner to watch *Love & Hip Hop*. Then she picked up the phone and started to dial.

***

I had a bit of jetlag once I was off the plane, but a blunt of blueberry Kush fixed that. I was looking for the outside terminal and once there, I saw the twins built like fucking Vin Diesel out of *The Fast and the Furious*. Both favored Jackie Chan in the face, but there was a difference to them. Once had curly brunette hair in a ponytail. The other twin had darker hair, with a Superman swirl in the front, also in a ponytail. They were both young, and I could tell they were both packing. They had a sign that read Mr. Monroe, of course, that was me.

So, I learned Milk Marie is in a room directly next to an empty room. She has access to that room as well. On a just in case level. She hadn't revealed to him she was here yet. The plan was that Milk Marie was flattered by Ken Chew's visit, and just felt the urge to come early etc., etc.

Walking up to them, I realized they both were only part Chinese. "You guys ready to go?" I said to them. They both looked at each other. I shook my head. I was guessing they couldn't speak English, "So, you guys don't speak English."

"Hell yes, we speak English. We just like fucking with people," the one with the brunette hair said. "See, if you don't say nothing, people assume you just don't speak English. Works great on chics," he said, opening the car door to a German Mercedes. By the way, I'm Ying and this is my brother, Yang." Ying pointed to his twin brother with the darker hair. As we got into the Benz, I realized they had to be seventeen or eighteen years old. I also realized they had been with the cartel since they were kids.

"So is Ying and Yang your real names?" I asked, already loving the view of Atlanta, the view being five college girls walking, all with big booties jiggling as we rode by. As we drove on, I realized we had to be in the downtown part of Atlanta. The buildings were beautiful, and the atmosphere smelled of success.

"Well," Yang said, "My name is William. And he used to go by Lil' Dave. But since we go everywhere together, as well as complete all of our missions together, they started calling us Ying and Yang, which stuck," Yang finished.

"I've never killed anyone without my brother present. All our kills are pretty much team efficient. No one has escaped a hit from us," Ying said.

"Not a soul," Yang said, his gray eyes beaming in mine, showing they were through.

Ying had the same gray eyes. I could have sworn I had seen the color before. Well, we were now parked. I followed them both out of the car to a nice downtown restaurant. You could smell the food before you even stepped inside. And the smells were wonderful. I was sleepy from the flight, but a lot hungrier. I could tell this was a hip restaurant and music venue on Edgewood Avenue. A local DJ, DJ Jay Cee who used to tour with Ludacris, spins almost every night of the week.

Outkast was blaring through the speakers. I ate a steak with A-1 Sauce, mashed potatoes, and a big drink called The Blue Motorcycle. The twins both ordered a huge chicken salad and drank Long Island Iced Teas. They were twins alright, but I could tell they were killers, by the way they scanned the room, and Ying was always in front while Yang took up the rear. I felt sorry for anyone wanting trouble, thinking they were average teenagers.

"Okay, this Ken Chew dude boring, boring," Ying said.

"Everything is business and most of the time, he takes the same route every day. Always with two Triad guards," Yang said.

"The only gap is his interest in Milk Marie. We watched him switch flights just to see her. Then he came back to Atlanta, which he only left for business," Yang stated. "So, whatever it is you and Milk Marie are supposed to handle, let us know our next move. Once you and Milk Marie are done, we got it from there," Yang said, finishing his salad. They were both using chopsticks as if they were just a spoon and a fork.

I realized just by this conversation they didn't have any idea about Wang feeling Ken Chew was Han. Nor did they know anything about the taking of the DNA. Obviously, that was for Wang's personal curiosity. As I saw things, Ying and Yang had been enjoying the sights of Atlanta, while waiting for orders to kill Ken Chew. I realized deep down I was not only here because of my loyalty to Han Che, but also my familiarity with Milk Marie.

Wang had us all doing his bidding, but after this, I was going to Italy. Rio didn't seem as appealing now. I chased after my mother, my father, and now I was chasing Han. I was tired of chasing ghosts. We ate our food while Ying and Yang explained the parts of Atlanta Ken Chew was always in. Cartel had their hands in whiskey, festivals, and most of downtown. Now I can see how Ken Chew, or someone, was trying to buy property in that area. It was their turf, and someone was trying to gain it, piece by piece.

We got to the Marriott, which wasn't far from the Four Seasons. The deal was, Milk Marie had a room in her name at the Four Seasons, and a room at the Marriott registered in her alias, Michelle Spencer. She could walk out of the Four Seasons and go behind a Dunkin Doughnuts and go right into the Marriott.

It was smart, but I felt Wang was being very paranoid. This wouldn't be a long trip, so it didn't matter. I wanted to go back to Shavonda, and our simple life in Virginia Beach. I had already sent her a text saying I loved and missed her.

"You got room 212. Milk Marie is in room 213, and we are in 209, which is across from both your rooms. Both motels are only booked for two more days. Once you leave, then we take it from here," Yang said, looking at his brother as to wonder if they left anything out or forgot anything. Once they gave me the room key, I went up with my Gucci carry-on luggage.

I got to the room and fell onto the bed. I stretched, then got up to look at the view from the second floor. It was nice. I unpacked and heard a door shut next door.

As soon as I heard Nicki Minaj, I knew it was Milk Marie. We had a door that connected to my room, but it had to be unlocked from the other side. I texted her, "What's up, Kat Stacks?" something I called her from time to time. Then my phone rang. "What's up, playa," I said, being sarcastic.

"Look, Malcolm is with my mom, the other kids are at camp. I just had to get away early. So, where are you, chilling with Patron?" she said with attitude.

"If you turn down that music, I could speak to you face-to-face. Since you like being put on a string and dunked in the water," I said.

"You're here? I thought you weren't coming for at least another day." She hung up and opened her side of the door. Then I opened mine and Milk Marie stood there, in an all-black Ralph Lauren collection jumpsuit, hands on her hips and waving me in her room. As I walked in, she had her Bluetooth playing music. She had crushed ice and Grey Goose on the coffee table in front of a plush white couch. I remembered what happened last time we sipped Goose. So, I asked if she had beer. She gave me a funny look and then got a Heineken out the fridge.

"Good thing that bellboy didn't pick up my flirting with him or this would seem awkward," she said, trying to push my buttons.

"Whatever, I am not getting into all that. But that outfit cost a grip. You got nice taste," I said.

"Honestly, Ken Chew bought this outfit," she said, eyeing me.

Now I was angry. "How the hell you going to meet with him already and not wait to see if everything is situated? This isn't the time for your way of wanting attention. The risk is too high. This isn't some fool from the club in the hood you kickin it with. Motherfucka is with the Triad and will kill you as quick as you blink," I said, downing the beer. "You want to fuck around, be my guest."

"It's not him," Milk Marie said, kicking off her shoes. She pulled off the Ralph Lauren jumpsuit and put on a long jersey, Michael Jordan's 23 jersey. It was one of my old ones from a year back. It looked sexy on her, like a dress, and she let her hair fall and sat on the couch crossing her legs. "Han is an asshole, a total complete asshole. Shit, he is handsome, but he looks like Danny Bowien," she said, rubbing her feet with one hand, drinking a glass of Grey Goose with the other.

I tried not to look at her legs, but she kept rubbing her foot. I was mad at myself wondering if she fucked this Ken Chew dude. I should not have cared, but the Chanel N° 5 that she wore was all over the room now, inviting me in. I was fighting the urge. It was time to be focused.

"So, you think just because the guy isn't an asshole, it's not Han? And who in the hell is Danny Bowien?"

"I mean, that's who this Ken Chew fellow looks like. You know, Danny Bowien, The Renegade Chef. You were thinking about getting into the restaurant business when we went to San Francisco that time," she said, remembering.

"Right, the restaurant was Mission Chinese Food. The chef that wears the designer clothing. But there is only one thing though," I said, remembering something.

"What? What's one thing?"

"Danny Bowien is Korean, not Chinese."

"Chinese, Korean, look… I'm just saying Ken Chew looks just like him, that's all. He looks nothing nor acts nothing like Han. I'll tell you that much." She curled up, sipping.

"Wang is going to be pissed! Did you at least get the DNA?" I said, knowing that was the only reason why we were even in Atlanta.

"Hold up. First of all, I volunteered to be bait, and secondly, I already told Wang. He was thrilled, the more I'm around Ken Chew, the better. Don't worry, I'll get the DNA. I was so pleased to have a man be attractive and buy me things," she said with a pout.

Chics like Milk Marie were all the same in the life of hustling. Thinking giving up the pussy is the key to everything. That shit is for suckers like Paul.

"Paul got you that expensive mini and God knows what else," I said to her ego.

"I mean, with Paul I had to be all Marilyn Monroe to get shit. Fendi, Prada, etc., and he sweat bullets every swipe of his credit card. Ken Chew just speaks it, and you have it," she said, grinning to herself like a girl who found out she was pregnant by a famous rapper.

"Oh, well do tell. I have to have my own intel as well, Milk," I said, rolling up a blunt, feeling a bit jetlagged from the flight.

"Well, I just told him I popped up in Atlanta early, that I had already been in touch with a modeling company in the Atlanta area. Asked if he would mind linking up. An hour later, I was picked up in front of the Four Seasons in a limousine. He made a fuss to get me an outfit. We went to a wine tasting, sit in afterwards. Then we ate some Chinese on the South side. But his two bodyguards were there the entire time."

"So, his security is tight by your observation?"

"Shit... let's just say if I had wanted to fuck him, I think the damn bodyguards would have been with us. Shit was corny, so I faked a headache and was brought back to the Four

Seasons. I went to my room for about thirty minutes, then watched my back best I could. Then I came to the Marriott. So, you meet the twins?" she asked me. I was sitting on the other end of the couch, realizing Milk Marie had closed the distance between us.

"Yeah, I met them. They seem pretty young, but they have been with the cartel since they were kids. This must really have Wang's attention going through all of this. I'm ready to get back, even though Atlanta is fly. The beach calling me," I said as I felt Milk Marie's toes rub my leg. Then I stood up as I smoked, brushing ashes off my jeans.

"Oh, it's like that? Boo, you don't have to worry about me saying nothing." She walked up to me in a perfumed cloud of Chanel N° 5 and Grey Goose on her breath. "No one around here but me and you," Milk Marie said, caressing the bulge in my pants.

I grabbed her hand and pulled it away. "Look, the other night we were drunk, and I can't play them games. I'll always have love for you though."

"But Yay, the other night was so good. I just want things to be the way they used to be. Why can't we do that?" Milk Marie said pissed, eyes watering. Regardless of how that night ended, the intimacy was undeniable.

"That's the problem with you, Milk. You just all about the moment, never the journey. My loyalty isn't that easily influenced. We got bad history, ma, so just leave it there," I said, seeing her disappointment. "Loyalty is rare, and it has to be respected. Therefore, you have no morals as a person," I said, walking back to my room. As I closed the door on my side of the room, I heard a glass shatter against it.

I already had a laptop computer in my room. As I turned it on, it welcomed me, then told me to type in my name. Once I did, pictures of Ken Chew flooded the screen, along with his two bodyguards. Each place the same. Lennox Book Company, a design company, Starbucks on the South Side, and then a last stop at the Museum of Art. Then obviously, his home base to sit before ending the day at Mason Fine Arts Gallery. All the pictures showed him never, ever leaving the bodyguards' sides. That's why Milk Marie was so important.

There were even pictures of Milk Marie going to Macy's with Ken Chew, but Wang already knew of them meeting. The twins were on top of Ken Chew's every move. I rubbed my eyes. The screen was bright in the dimly lit room. I kicked my wheat Timbs off and laid on the bed. So much talk about Ken Chew. I was told I get to see him tomorrow for myself, so I rested.

Fre$h

Chapter 13

Big Bad Wolf

My phone was buzzing like crazy, and I woke up aggravated. I didn't want to deal with Milk Marie's childish attitude. She had fucked Han, probably on some slut vendetta. Then once the gravity of what she did played guilt on her, she wanted a relationship. But my eyes were open. I got her off the streets. We had threesomes and the sex was fly, but all we did was play house. When it all boiled down, I couldn't trust her. I remember calling Patron right before I got to the house that night.

"Damn, it's late, homie. You okay?" Patron said yawning. "Lisa chewed me out about being drunk, so my ass be in the house. She finally sleep. I couldn't take another *Netflix* movie," he said giggling.

"I fucked up, bruh. Milk Marie slick ass got the dick tonight."

"I told you, either her or Taylor Swift were going to get to you. I've never messed with a white chic, but I heard they suck dick like they going to get a damn trophy," Patron said.

"Homie, I feel like shit. Shavonda be holding me down. I'm about to go crash, the walk got me tired," I said, fumbling for my keys.

"Look, just go to Atlanta, handle your business, and come back focused. Just try not to have her in Atlanta. I would go, but after Spain, Lisa giving me hell. Hold it down, homie. Broke niggas make noise," Patron said.

"Rich niggas make moves," I said, hanging up. I was shaken out of my daydream by someone knocking on the door. I pulled out the Desert Eagle Ying gave me. I wouldn't dare take a gun on a plane. I didn't want to go through what Juelz

Santana from Dipset went through, and that's my dude. I put my eye against the peephole to see Ying and he looked pissed. I opened the door.

"Come to my room now, we got a problem," he said, walking back to 209. I slipped on my nine, tucked my gun, looked up and down the hallway and went into the twin's room.

When I shut the door behind me, I thought I was in another world. Computers were everywhere, and there were several flat screens mounted on the walls. It looked like the fucking CIA headquarters.

"Okay, so what you're looking at is all our eyes and ears on Ken Chew. "It's um," he looked at his Rolex, "two pm and Milk Marie has had breakfast with him, as well as went to the Museum an hour ago. She doing all this shit on her own. Yang is out now keeping an eye out. Yay, me and my brother never separate. Your baby momma acting like a brat," Ying said, tapping keys on the keyboard.

"Tell me something I don't know. So, is she at least wearing the bracelet?" I said, looking at the monitors watching the Museum, still in view.

"Yes, I know that for sure. There is a tracking device on it and once it is around her wrist, it activates. I also have sound, though Yang has to be within a certain radius to pick it up." Ying said, "But Ken Chew seems to be in a bit of hot water," enhancing the focus on the museum.

"So, are they still in the museum?" I asked, pacing back and forth. Milk Marie was pissing me off.

"No, but I know they still in there, via the tracking device, so let's just hope she got something up her sleeve," Ying said, opening a Pepsi. I rolled a blunt and as I passed it to Ying, my phone rang.

"Hello?" I said.

"Seemi, hey baby. Um, I don't try to bother you. I mean, I know how busy you are," Aunt Nancy said.

"I'm never too busy for you, Aunt Nancy. Just got some business in Atlanta, and I'll be back. What's up?"

"Well, I hope it has nothing to do with a Ken Chew. Damn cops came to my door for me to tell you to stay away from this guy. Listen, Yay, we need to talk," Aunt Nancy was saying. I was too busy looking at several screens. One with Milk Marie and Ken Chew coming out of the museum flanked, of course, by both his bodyguards.

"Look, I have to get back to what I was doing, Auntie, but did the guy have a bald head, salt and pepper hair?" I said praying she said no.

"Why, yes. Listen, we need to talk, son," Aunt Nancy said. Even though I was her nephew, she raised me. So, Aunt Nancy called me son a lot more than nephew.

"Aunt Nancy, I have to go. Listen, I'll call you soon as I get back," I said, hanging up.

"Yo, we good, Yay? You look like you want to kill somebody," Ying said, looking at the monitors.

"If the chase come, a lot of motherfuckas about to feel my heat. We got to wrap this shit up. I got to get back to E-City," I said, ready to body something.

"Yo, are you seeing this shit? Looks like she going to pull it off," Ying said as we both watched the screen as Milk Marie palmed Ken Chew's ass. Then smoothly removing the bracelet, she pinched his ass at the same time as she poked him with the needle. Before you could blink, the bracelet was back on her wrist. Ken Chew returned her gesture by pinching her ass back before getting in the limousine. I could hear Yang in Ying's earpiece saying, "That's one scandalous bitch, man. Shorty cold-blooded. Anyway, following them back to the Four Seasons."

"Trust me, if anyone know, I know. She straight savage. I wouldn't trust her to make me a peanut butter and jelly sandwich," I said, making both Ying and Yang laugh. Apparently, Yang could hear us as well.

"Well, at least you two get to leave now. We been here like three weeks following this clown. I'm ready to kill, so I can go to Italy with my brother and Mum," Ying said, feeling his and Yang's stakeout was coming to an end. But I was thinking about Officer Dickerson. He fucked up going to my aunt's home. He was indeed a dead man!

***

Meanwhile, little did I know, Dickerson had issues of his own. He was in Atlanta at that very moment riding in a black Lexus with mirror tint, shaking his head at the envelope that made him read the contents over and over again. He had an idea that it was a possibility, but all this time he was in shock. The visit with Ms. Baxter made him dig into his past. The paperwork in his hand was twenty-four years old, and he was soon to leave the E-City Police Department for good. Before his flight, he went in his garage and dug through the past. Now he knew the meaning of skeletons in your closet.

He punched the steering wheel. "Fuck, fuck, fuck!" Then he looked up at the ceiling. "I have to do this. I'm sorry." Dickerson was briefed once he landed in Atlanta. The ATF agent gave it to him straight.

"Okay, Corey, you are a ghost. You volunteered to take this assignment. If you succeed, you're in. If you fail, then just be happy with your spotted record. You will still draw a pension. Agent White straightened his tie, looking like Tommy Lee Jones from the *Men in Black* movie. "I've lost three agents trying to do what you're trying to pull. If you can find any-thing dirty on this Ken Chew, we want him. He is the new kid on the block for the Triad. And he has been a thorn in my side in Atlanta for three months now. Obviously, he's bullying property and triple the growth on said property."

Then Agent White pulled out files. "Lennox Book Com-pany, a design company, and the list goes on. You find any dirt, I mean enough dirt that collects under a fingernail, we can get this guy. Now we think the museum is dirty, but it's historic. So, we have to have something concrete. You want to be an agent and play with the big boys? This is your shit. You get made, and we don't know you. We never had this conversation. So, are you sure you have found a connection to Ken Chew?" Agent White said, hoping this prick could pull off what three agents couldn't.

Agent White knew about the rumors of extortion, money laundering, even tampering with evidence. But on paper, he was cleaner than a baby's ass. Besides, you need scum to trap scum sometimes. Agent White had a feeling the cartel wasn't liking the Triad so close to this area one bit. The higher-ups wanted results, or his department would be shut down. He was getting old and after He's disappearance, Agent White had al-most given up, until Ken Chew popped up on his radar. If Dickerson could find something good, if not, he was expend-able. Agent White could really not have cared less. He just wanted results.

"I have a connection, and I will get you what you need," Dickerson said. He snapped out of his thoughts as he saw a pretty white girl get out of a limousine to the Four Seasons.

Dickerson wanted to make agent in order to wipe away the speculation down at the precinct. Once he had his mole tell him of Yay's interest in Ken Chew, he couldn't pass up the opportunity. He just hoped Yay would stay out of his way.

Then too, for the gun was sitting cozy in his safe. But though he could get more money out of Yay if this was a success, he would take Yay's ass down too. He said out loud to himself in the car, "Agent Dickerson." Yes, he liked the sound of that. He drove off, following three car lengths behind the limousine.

***

Yang was coming off the elevator to the room, just as Milk Marie had doubled back from the Four Seasons. Once Yang was in the room, Ying handed him a Pepsi. Then for the first time, I paid attention to the room. Pizza boxes and Pepsi cans were everywhere.

"When was the last time you guys slept?" I said, watching them look at each other curiously.

"Hell, I don't know. Well, your girl is a mess, but she got it," Yang said.

"Where is she?" I said, ready to get the bracelet to the twins and go kill this Dickerson clown.

"She was a few paces behind me, maybe she is in her room," Ying said. Then there was a knock on the door. Ying got up to open the door. Milk Marie burst in with tears pouring down her face. I hadn't seen her like this since the warehouse incident.

"It's him! It's fucking him! I want out right now. This is some fucked-up *Twilight Zone* shit." Milk Marie said, looking dashing in a Ralph Lauren collection, snug one-piece dress. It had purple, white, yellow, red and blue stripes. She looked like a delicious candy cane. Her Puma sneakers matched the dress with a yellow purse. She was holding on to me, shaking violently. Yang had gotten some bottled water out of the fridge. I had to pry her off me, sit her down, and get her to calm down.

"Here drink some of this and take a deep breath. I need you to breathe," I said, as she took big gulps of the water. Once she calmed down some, I said, "Okay, now tell us what happened." Me and Yang were facing her. Ying was still at the desk looking at all of the monitors.

"Okay, so, I was pissed about last night. I left the room and went to the Four Seasons. I woke up, dressed, and called Ken Chew. He picked me up in the limo. We made a few stops, but once we got to the museum, his demeanor changed."

"What do you mean, his demeanor changed?" I said.

"He was talking about never allowing anyone to get close to him." She stared off as if daydreaming. "Then he brushed my hair across my face and gave me a fucked-up smile. Then he said, 'But you are my weakness, and I can't afford to be weak.' And just like that, he was back to being attractive and sweet. But for that short while," she looked at me with tears in her eyes, "I could have sworn it was Han talking to me. I was so shaken. I felt like he did it because acting that nice was boring to him," she said then took the bracelet off and handed it to Yang. "I'm done. Shit creeping me out."

"Okay. We got what we came for. I'm down with getting out of here. Maybe all the shit that's going on and Wang putting shit in your head." I said, noticing something on the screen. It was a gold Lexus 400. I kept thinking, where *did I know the car from*?

"There isn't shit in my head. Yay, please listen to me. I know. My fucking skin is still crawling," she said, still breathing hard.

"Shit, man, you would think she talking about the Big Bad Wolf," Yang said, loading his .45 Glock. I was too busy looking at the screen.

"Ying, who the fuck is that? I know that car, and the limousine is back at the museum," I said, tapping the screen.

"Oh, that's some lawyer scumbag. He drops in on Ken Chew from time to time, usually at the Starbucks," Ying said.

"Yeah, we got intel that the lawyer is behind the property buying and that's a fine ass chic with him," Yang said, loading another gun.

"What the fuck! That's Shavonda! What the fuck is Shavonda doing here?" I felt like the room was spinning. Then I looked at Milk Marie, and I pulled my gun out. I pointed it at her head because I was tired of the betrayal. "Why the fuck is Shavonda here, Milk? You better not have nothing to do with this shit," I said, not even blinking. I was ready to take her head off.

"Yay, what are you doing? Yes, I'm beyond jealous that bitch has you, but I don't know why she is here," Milk Marie cried.

"What's going on, guys? Did we miss something?" Ying said as Yang was standing beside me, whispering in my ear.

"If she dirty, she dead, but right now we got to find out why your shorty here. Okay? We supposed to have our guns pointed at the other guys," Yang said to me.

"Look. Only thing I know, before we left, Larry called me. He said he wanted to talk, but I told him I was going out of town on business," Milk Marie said, crying as I cocked the hammer back on the gun. "I never told him where I was going. Then he said no need to tell anybody he called."

I lowered the gun, then I addressed Ying and Yang. "He was a lawyer for the cartel. His name is Larry Lawrence." I took a deep breath. "I need to know all the artillery you have." Yang smiled at me and opened the closet and there was an arsenal of guns, vests, silencers, and small walkie talkies.

"I've been in this fucking room for three weeks. I'm ready to put in work," Yang said, putting on a vest and then putting his shirt back on. I was doing the same, while Ying was pulling an M-16 out the closet. I had grabbed another Desert Eagle. I was ready to kill anything moving. Then I thought about the sample of DNA in the bracelet.

"What about the DNA?" I said, walking back up to the screen watching Larry escort Shavonda in the Museum.

"The guy at the front desk is one of our handlers. He will next-day it to Wang. Kendrick was placed at the front desk, just in case Ken Chew ever got wise to Milk Marie switching rooms," Ying said. He obviously always had his best on. I looked at Milk Marie and felt no remorse for pulling the gun on her. She seemed to be reading my mind.

"No need for any hard feelings. I know because of our past, you feel you can't trust me, but do what you got to do. Just don't forget Malcolm needs his father," she said.

"After we leave, I don't know the outcome. So, if I were you, I'd get the hell out of here." I looked up at Ying and Yang. They were both strapped to the teeth without hesitation. I had no idea what I was going to do, but I knew I had to act on my impulse. "You two ready to go all out, not knowing the outcome?" I said, rechecking my guns.

"We are Cartel, Yay," Ying said, slapping the magazine in his M-16.

"Always will be Cartel," Yang said, swinging a Mossberg pump over his shoulder.

"Then let's go kill, as you said earlier, the Big Bad Wolf." I said, gritting my gold teeth walking out the door. My plan was to just go straight to the Museum and play it from there. The twins had a black van they were going to use after they cleaned up Ken Chew. Seemed the appropriate time to use it.

As we pulled off, Ying was driving, and Yang was in the passenger seat. Yang then looked at me in the backseat of the van, "Okay, we running up on this fool, right? But why are we running up strapped like Rambo? Your girl, Shavonda, seemed to be just walking up the steps on her own with this Larry Lawyer dude," Yang said.

I saw Ying's eyes meet mine in the rearview mirror. Before I could speak up, he did. "Because, dear brother, when you were trying to calm Yay here from popping Milk Marie's melon, you didn't see what he saw. I picked up on it when he looked closer at the screen," Ying said, getting closer to the museum.

"And what did you two see?" Yang said, lighting a blunt of Moonrock.

"That Larry was walking beside her with a gun in Shavonda's back. He was hiding it the best he could, but she wasn't going with him of her own free will. Now they went in the Museum. Why, I don't know. But all I know right now all our players are in the Museum," I said as the aroma filled the can.

"So, that is pretty much the element of surprise? We walk in a public museum and go straight *Menace II Society* on that ass, not knowing what's waiting for us?" questioned Yang, passing the Moonrock to Ying.

"Don't forget possibly to die a horrible death because technically, South Side, where the museum is located is a Triad area." Yang said, passing me the blunt of Moonrock.

"Yes," I said, hitting the blunt, "pretty much."

"I like it. I was itching to get the cobwebs off my heat," Yang said, kissing the Mossberg Pump. We were on our way to kill the Big Bad Wolf, but we were definitely not three little pigs.

Chapter 14

I'll Huff and I'll Puff...

Milk Marie was still trying to get her head wrapped around the way Yay had acted. The last person that put a gun in her face was Han. Now her own baby daddy. She vowed the next person to do that would definitely die by her hands. It seems everyone she fucked seemed to turn on her.

She was loose and extremely flirty, she knew this. She tried her best to be the bait to make things better, but now Shavonda was somehow in danger. Yay was going to be Shavonda's knight in shining armor and not hers. It hurt, but the betrayal of what happened with Han was too much for Yay to forgive. Her phone rang, interrupting her thoughts.

"Hello," she said walking towards the door.

"Damn, about time someone picked up their phone. Look, where is Yay?" Gucci Swagg said. "He isn't answering the phone."

"He is gone to the Museum on the South Side to get Shavonda. Han..." then Milk Marie started stuttering. "Um, I mean, t-this Ken Chew guy we think has Shavonda against her will," Milk Marie said, beginning to open the door.

"We, me and P-Funk, are already in Atlanta. Patron was acting real weird about where Yay was, so we came out here ourselves. Where are you?" Gucci Swagg said, loading up the 45 Glock.

"I'm at the Marriott, room 209. Please come get me. I do not want to be alone," Milk Marie said.

"We aren't too far from there because I use to boost cars up here. Ask her is it near the Four Seasons?" P-Funk said, driving with a .357 in his lap.

"It is by the Four Seasons, Milk Marie?" Gucci Swagg asked her.

"Yes, there's a Dunkin Doughnuts is the middle."

"Okay, I'll be waiting out front." Then she hung up. When Milk Marie opened the door, she was hit hard in the face with the butt of a gun. She fell to the floor, and someone shut the door behind her. She felt a knot swelling right above her left eye. Once Milk Marie looked up, she was in utter shock.

"Hey, bitch, did you miss me?" Paul said, sneering at her in a dingy suit. He smelled of booze like he had been binge drinking. Paul pointed the gun at her. "Got your baby daddy to kick my ass, and then you go off to Atlanta with him." He cocked the gun. "If I can't have you, shit, then no one can. Now, like a doctor says, 'Say ah… ah," he said, kicking her. She didn't understand at first. Then he squatted down next to her on the phone with spit flying from his mouth. "Open your mouth, bitch. I know you know how to do that." He put the .44 Bulldog up to her lips.

Now Milk Marie was terrified at first, but then she thought of all the shit she had been through. Thinking back to the guy that left her on the highway. Every man that ever abused her. Not to mention, just minutes ago, Yay had his Desert Eagle to her face. Something happened and she wasn't afraid at all. Somehow, she became calm, and she did what came natural. She licked her lips seductively and opened wide. Paul pushed the big barrel of the .44 Bulldog in her mouth. She stated sucking on it like she had sucked his pockets dry for almost a year.

Milk Marie could tell he was enjoying what she was doing, because he started rubbing his crotch. "Oh, you like that, bitch? Yeah, deep throat it, baby. I think I'll fuck you before I kill you," Paul said, pulling the gun out of her mouth while unzipping his pants.

"Anything you say, daddy," she said, wiggling her plump ass and bending over. The Ralph Lauren dress with the rainbow stripes was riding up her backside, exposing her bright pink Victoria's Secret thong. Milk Marie was waiting for her opportunity, looking over her shoulder, shaking her ass. Then there was a loud knock on the door.

"Milk Marie, are you here? We got to get moving," Gucci Swagg was saying from the other side of the door.

Paul looked back with his little manhood dangling out his zipper. "Oh, bitch, you got more men coming to your room?" Paul said, still gripping the .44 Bulldog in one hand. His other hand was on Milk Marie's ass cheek.

She then kicked him right in his dick, as hard as she could. He dropped the gun, crumbling to the floor.

"Fuck you, stupid bitch!" Paul screamed out, enraged and balled up on the floor holding his dick. She then grabbed the gun and ran to the door and opened it. Gucci Swagg and P-Funk stepped inside, with guns drawn, both looking at each other, eyebrows raised.

"Yo, Milk, why is some white guy who looks like a broke Mark Walberg, holding his little dick and rolling around on the floor?" P-Funk said, his .357 blue steel, long-nosed gun looking like the gun out of the Clint Eastwood *Dirty Harry* movies.

"I know you and Yay at odds, but this is too weird. We got to get to the Museum," Gucci Swagg said, 45 Glock cocked and ready to rock.

"Fucking bitch! Both of you, this fool tried to rape me!" Then Milk Marie grabbed a pillow off one of the twin's beds, put it to Paul's head. *BOOM, BOOM*

She let off two shots with the .44 Bulldog. The pillow quieted the blast, feathers floated all in the air, mixed with Paul's brain matter and blood all over the floor.

"Damn, Milk Marie! What the fuck, ma?" Gucci Swagg said, shaking his head at what was left of Paul.

She looked at Paul and spit on his body, then kicked his lifeless body. "I will never fuck another mothafucka that trips about buying a two-thousand-dollar dress ever again. Now, let's go. Yay needs us," Milk Marie said, walking out the door as if a corpse wasn't lying in the middle of the room.

P-Funk just shrugged his shoulders and said, "Yay be fucking some crazy bitches."

"No doubt! Let's bounce, I got a feeling more bodies 'bout to drop," Gucci Swagg said as they closed the door to go find Yay.

***

Officer Dickerson was sitting in the all-black Lexus with rims. He hated the car since it made him look like a dope boy. But after he landed in Atlanta, the ATF was not spending money on an operation that didn't exist. So, he picked it out of the federal impound and it was either that, or a pink Honda with rims. Some girl was selling opium and got the customized pink car. So, Dickerson was stuck with the Lexus. At least the drug dealer that owned it had a little class.

He was calling Agent White, because he just saw some guy that looked like Bob Hope in an expensive suit. That female with the huge booty was walking up the Museum steps. He noticed just a glimpse of Bob Hope's arm around her waist, the other pushing what looked to be a gun in her side.

"Agent White here."

"Sir, it seems a female is being held at gunpoint inside the museum. Now Ken Chew and his goons are in there. Permission to engage on the situation," he was saying, not noticing the van passing him, going around a building to park.

"Dickerson, have you seen any drugs, or any money exchange hands?" Agent White said aggravated. He needed results, not some random kidnapping.

"No sir, but whatever is going on, I'm sure Ken Chew is in the middle of it. Now may I engage?" Dickerson said, tired of Agent White's bullshit.

"No. Do not, I repeat do not engage. Unless you see cash or drugs exchanged. Do you understand?" Agent White said with authority.

"Yes. Understood." Then he hung up. He decided to go in and have a look around, since he was doing an operation that was off the books. Dickerson would get results and he hoped Yay got his message. If not, he would regret that he would go down as well. He exited the Lexus and walked across the street as a few people were walking out. Once he passed a few expensive artifacts, he noticed more people leaving. He assumed they were closing. He saw Ken Chew and his two bodyguards in front of a huge painting of the Mona Lisa. The guy that looked like Bob Hope was still with the pretty light-skinned girl. Looked as if Ken Chew was not too happy with his presence.

Dickerson saw a utility closet and ducked inside, giving him a perfect view of Ken Chew and the gang. So, he would wait to see if he could get the dirt he needed.

***

We had pulled alongside a building two blocks from the museum. Ying and Yang were right on my heels. We were greeted by a small wave of people. Once we got to the entrance, two men in identical suits who looked like janitors stopped us from going inside. "Sorry guys, the Museum is closing early today. Come back nine am tomorrow," one of them said. A lot of people had come out, but I didn't see Larry or Shavonda. The limousine was parked on the side of the museum, as well as the Lexus. So, Shavonda was still in there.

"So, there is no one else in there? Because I think my lady may be in there," I said, not blinking, still walking towards the two guys.

"Sir, other than the owner and his associates, the Museum is closed," the other janitor looking fellow said.

I pulled out my Desert Eagle and pointed it at one of the guys. Ying and Yang had their guns out on the other guy. "I'm only going to say his once. If you don't want to die, then you had better leave."

The two guys looked at each other, then back at me and the twins. They both ripped their museum badges off. "Fuck this. They don't pay me enough to die," one of them said.

"Yeah, the art in there is bullshit anyway," the other guy replied as they both took off down the steps, not even looking back. We shut the doors and were walking towards a big statue of a dinosaur.

"Okay, Ying, you go left. Yang, you go right. I'm going in a straight line. Stay close, because they are in here," I said as I walked, watching both Ying and Yang vanish. I walked for a short while. The Museum was huge. Despite what the janitor guy said, some of the artifacts were quite nice. There was a cannon from 1808, a gun in a case with Billy the Kid's signature on it, and I figured a lot of these were things Ken Chew purchased for himself.

There was a huge figure of Genghis Khan. Then, I heard voices. There was a huge picture of *Mona Lisa*, and everyone was standing in front of it. Two big statues of Samaria Warriors with swords raised in victory was keeping me hidden from sight. The gun was more visible now. I leaned on the statue

136

while listening to them talk. Ken Chew so far sounded pissed off.

"Can you fucking explain to me why this pretty young lady is in my museum? Then, I want to understand why I still have a briefcase with a million in it that's supposed to go to buying the land the Whiskey Festival is hosted on?" Ken Chew said back to everyone still admiring the painting.

"Ken Chew, this has more to do with you inviting Ms. Johnson here. Damn it, I can't believe you were arrogant enough to contact her," Larry said, releasing his grip on Shavonda.

"I would remind you to watch your tongue, Mr. Lawrence, for I have no patience for fools on my midst," Ken Chew said, turning around with a Glock .40 with a beam on it directly in the middle of Larry's forehead.

Larry put his gun in his holster and started stuttering like a schoolgirl. "L-listen to me, we don't have time for this. N-now this is Yay's girl, and what I got out of her is, the Cartel thinks you're Han."

Ken Chew started laughing, and then the bodyguards joined in. Larry seemed annoyed by Ken Chew's arrogance.

"Not only that, but I believe that Milk Marie only went along with your advances, trying to find a way to prove you're not who you say you are. This shit is serious and all over some pussy," Larry said, running his hands through his hair.

Then, just like that, Ken Chew stopped laughing because he was thinking back to when she pinched his ass. Ken Chew felt himself, but wasn't sure if the little sting he felt was the work of Milk Marie. She had given him that bomb head and then he couldn't resist telling her how weak he was for her. She seemed afraid, and it turned him on. Now he felt contacting her was indeed a mistake.

"Okay, so if Ms. Johnson is an issue, why the hell you kidnap this tasty piece of ass?" Ken Chew said, looking her up and down. Yay has truly stepped it up since Milk Marie. But if Milk Marie had indeed did something to him, then of course, a trade had to be made. Maybe Larry was smarter than he looked.

"Because where there is fire, there is smoke. I had contacted Ms. Johnson, but I didn't have a chance to question her. She said she was going out of town for business. So, I follow this one and tell her Yay is in trouble. Of course, I tell her I'm his lawyer, and it's urgent I speak to him. She said he is on some wild goose chase. Once she tells me everything, I snatch her. She seemed to be… um," Larry said, touching her long hair "having a naughty little dinner at an expensive restaurant."

"Don't touch me, you lying bastard. Where is Yay? Just let me go, this has nothing to do with me," she said, looking gorgeous in a silver Iris Van Herpen dress. It was tight fitting, but Yay wandered why she was dressed so eloquently. Something wasn't right, and he felt this was the time to strike. He saw Ying behind a statue of a naked woman with no arms. To his right, Yang was squatting down by a big glass casing of elephant bones.

"Oh, take her with you, and I'll get down to the bottom of this. Somebody is going to bleed," Ken Chew said, adjusting his tie paired with his five-thousand-dollar suit.

I met eyes with both Ying and Yang as they never took their eyes off me. I nodded to both of them, and they understood.

"Someone will bleed for this, I was just thinking the same thing." I said, coming out of my hiding place with both Desert Eagles cocked and at the ready. Ken Chew's coward ass got behind Shavonda. "All I want is my lady and we can call it a day, gentlemen. Or I promise you, someone will bleed."

"Well, Mr. Yay, is it? I'm guessing this tasty bitch is your property? However, a man must keep his women in check." Ken Chew pointed a chrome .45 to Shavonda's back. Running the gun through Shavonda's hair, he continued. "Trust me, her presence here was not my idea, but another one of your acquaintances, I believe has something that belongs to me. Now, you bring that little white bitch to me, we trade, and everyone goes home," Ken Chew said, backing up a few paces with Shavonda.

I, myself, kept inching forward, watching Ying a few feet back from one of the bodyguards. I had no idea what would happen, but I felt if he left with Shavonda, I would never see her again. No, we had to stop this and stop it now.

"Not the plan, playboy. Now last time, let her go," I said, watching Ying make his move. He swung the M-16 and let it spray.

Larry dropped, bullets tearing his right leg off. His screams filled the Museum as the bodyguard felt the wrath of the M-16. I was not taking my eyes off Ken Chew. Then the last of Yang's Mossberg Pump roared, catching the other bodyguard off guard but somehow, he still got a shot off and hit Yang. But Yang seemed to be okay while holding his now bloody right hand. Larry was still on the floor screaming. I put two shots in him, and for a second, there was total silence.

"As I was saying, let her go or you're next," I said, still smelling the gunpowder from the shots I gave Larry's punk ass.

Nervous, with Shavonda still in front of him, Ken Chew's left arm wrapped around her and his right hand on the chrome .45 to her head. All of a sudden, a door slammed, and a voice came from behind all of us. Ying, Yang, and I had all our guns pointed at Ken Chew.

"All of you are under arrest. Put your weapons on the floor and your hands in the air." Dickerson then cocked his police issued firearm, "I will not ask you again, gentlemen."

"Well, I'll be damned. Now it's a party, but Mr. Policeman, where dear sir, is your back-up?" Ken Chew said, making a point while still pressing the gun to Shavonda's head.

"Guns down now!" Dickerson yelled, then two shots boomed through the Museum, dropping Dickerson. He, in turn, pulled his trigger. The bullet hit Ken Chew and the .45 chrome barked, taking Shavonda's head off.

Ying hit Ken Chew on the head with the butt of the M-16. Everyone was still figuring out where the shot came from. Then Gucci Swagg appeared with his .45 smoking. He then kicked Dickerson's gun away and kicked him in the face. P-Funk was not far behind with his .357 in hand.

Gucci Swagg and P-Funk looked around at all the bodies. Then there was silence, other than Ken Chew and Dickerson on the floor groaning. Everyone, like Tupac, had all eyes on me. I walked up to Shavonda's body and fell down beside her. I let out a terrifying yell.

"Ahhhhh, Ahhhhhh!" I wiped my eyes, then I heard hysterical laughter. I realized it was coming from Ken Chew.

With blook spilling from his mouth he said, "Déjà vu, I guess. Huh, Yay? Once again, you are in my way. My piece of shit father still has your services from the grave." Ken Chew looked up at me and smiled a very evil smile. Now I knew what Milk Marie meant. This was not Ken Chew, but Han.

"After my unfortunate swim, I was rescued by a crew of fishermen. I killed every last one of them. I mean, I couldn't have anyone exposing I was alive. It took me three months, but the plastic surgery was successful," he said, spitting up more blood.

"Then of course, you killed the guy behind the surgery," I said, wiping my eyes as Shavonda's blood oozed on the floor.

"Naturally, and I healed. I made myself look more of the Triad culture. I was going to destroy my father's ventures by buying him out. His land, businesses, and I was actually getting things accomplished. Larry came on board, so in order to know he was loyal, I got him to poison Han Che." Then he coughed and laughed. "I even went to the funeral. Just another Chinese face."

"Why is he telling us all this?" Ying said, still holding the M-16 trained on his head.

"Because," Yang said, wrapping up his hand with a piece of shirt he ripped off one of the bodyguards, "he is dying, so why not? The cough shows the bullet hit a lung," Yang was satisfied with the wrapping of his hand. Then Yang took all the phones off everyone, bodyguards, even Larry. All of their wallets were taken.

I walked to a curtain hanging on the walls. I wrapped Shavonda's body up because I was not leaving her here.

"You stuck your nose in things that had nothing to do with you. So, you reap the karma of meddling in my affairs," Han said, coughing and spitting up blood.

"Your father once told me a man makes his own choices and accepts the outcome of his karma," I said, walking up to the statue of the two Samurai warriors. I knew without knowing, and I felt Han Che was with me. I pulled one of the long swords from the statue. It was heavy, but it was in good condition. Then I could hear Han Che's voice from my dream.

"Yayo Sun, all enemies must be exterminated. This is the balance that has to be kept. They are not who they say they are."

I walked up to Han and raised the sword. Then I hacked away at his neck while he was still alive. Everyone thought I had gone mad. Once the head was severed, I ripped another piece of curtain and wrapped his head in it.

"What the fuck, Yay, man? You on some *Silence of the Lambs* shit?" Gucci Swagg said as he and P-Funk still couldn't believe what they just saw. "We need to bounce. Milk Marie is in the truck. Some dude named Paul tried to rape and kill her." Gucci Swagg kicked Dickerson's body. "What we do with this clown? He a cop."

"Wait! Wait! Yay, please listen to me. I'm your father!" Dickerson said. He was shot but seemed like he could make it. I put the gun to his head.

"This is not the time to test me," I said, with Han's blood all on me. Shit, if they wanted DNA, I had it all over me.

"Shirley and I dated years ago. I never knew if she was really pregnant. I was just getting in the academy back then. Anyway," he tried to speak, groaning on the floor, "Shirley was tired of me not wanting to commit, so she dated a guy named Dexter. Once on the force, I tried to get her back, but your aunt Nancy drove me away. Said Dexter was helping her with the baby."

The shit was becoming too much for me, and I was beyond dumbfounded.

"Then what happened to Mom, you piece of shit? Why was I given up for adoption?" I said, kicking him. "Why?" I yelled.

"Dexter and your mom went on a trip to New York. Nancy had just gotten married back then and was on her honeymoon, when your mom and Dexter died in a car crash. I still have no idea who was babysitting you when all of this occurred. I think it was some friends of Dexter's. The state picked you up when no one came to claim you. I'm sorry, son," Dickerson said.

"Don't call me son. You're not my father. Did you know this when you were fucking extorting me? Disown me, then come for my money." I kicked him again.

"No, no! The case with Mr. Jackson is how I was able to do research. I found out who your aunt was, your only living relative."

"So, that's why you went by Aunt Nancy's house? You were investigating Ken Chew and I bet you were planning to take me down with him," I said, suspicious.

"No," Dickerson said lying, then he reached in his bloody shirt. Everyone put their guns on him, "Wait, wait, it's only a piece of paper. Jesus," he said, his bloody hands shaking and holding a yellow envelope. I opened it and it was an old paternity test dated twenty-five years ago. It had Shirley Baxter's name on it, as well as a Corey T. Dickerson. Test results were ninety-nine-point-nine percent positive.

"Why didn't you show Aunt Nancy this?" I said, trying to control my emotions. I felt like I was in a damn movie.

"Your aunt knew, but she didn't want me in the way. She said Shirley and Dexter were happy," Dickerson said sadly.

I took my necklace out with the long Figaro chain dangling. On the end was a gold frame with a black and white picture of my mom. Dickerson smiled briefly at the picture.

"I took that after we graduated. It's in the yearbook. I was a photographer for the school," he said.

"I thought our life was weird being half-British and half-Chinese. I mean, really, what Chinese guy speaks the way we do? It's bloody weird, that's what it is," Ying said.

"Ying, shut up. We know our father, and we will not discuss that here," Yang said. Then his eyes went to Yay. "Sorry to break up your family reunion, but three people are on the floor dead. One is missing a head."

I shoved the papers in my pocket. It was time to get the hell out of here. I guess Wang didn't have to wait for DNA. Then Gucci Swagg started kicking Dickerson viciously.

"Give me that, you sneaky mothafucka!" Gucci Swagg said, taking a small phone from Dickerson on the floor. He was reading the text messages. He looked down at Dickerson then kicked him again. "We got to go, not now, but right now. This mothafucka is a fed, man. Clown texting Agent White that money and possibly drugs are present. 'Hurry!' Then gave the location of the museum," Swagg said, spitting on Dickerson. "I hate fucking cops. Not only that, he fed."

"Okay Ying, get Shavonda and Yang, grab that head. Gucci Swagg and P-Funk, torch the place." Everyone did as I asked as smoke filled the Museum. Ying and Yang headed out the back to the van. Gucci Swagg and P-Funk ran up to me.

"Let's go, bruh. This place is going up," he said.

"I'm right behind you now go, get out of here," I said. They both looked at me, then at Dickerson on the floor and started to leave. "P-Funk, grab the briefcase from Larry." Once they were gone, I turned my attention to Dickerson. I couldn't believe this piece of shit was my father, but this guy was a stranger to me. He was only trying to buy time to stay alive. I was of my mother's bloodline and not his.

I raised the Desert Eagle to his face. There was so much I wanted to ask, but I was a grown ass man now. So, nothing he said mattered.

"For what it's worth, Shirley was a great woman," he said, coughing because of the smoke.

"Sorry I cannot say the same for you as a man. Do me a favor and tell Han hello in hell. I'm sure you won't see Mom where you are going." I then emptied the clip into the guy that was my father. Every shot was for every birthday, every tear, and every disappointment. Sadly, now me and Han were, unfortunately, the same. We had both killed our fathers, but I also felt like Han Che. I had lost my woman to a feud. A feud over revenge where there is no understanding, nothing can be understood. As I walked out the museum, I felt complete and empty at the same time.

Fre$h

Chapter 15

Unfinished Business

I paid for Shavonda's funeral. I heard a lot of her family attended. I, myself, did not go. Of course, I had my reasons.

After everything was said and done, months had gone by. I ended up getting a condo on the beach of Southern Shores. It was a very spacious condo on the outskirts of Virginia. Being on the beach is the only place I felt free when I was going through something. I would watch the waves for hours and Patron would brag about the way he planned to get money. But messing with chics didn't give him the edge I had. Yet and still, we were brothers from another mother.

As I stood at the pane glass window with my all-white Gucci linen on, Gucci loafers, and gold Gucci shades, I watched the waves thinking of those times long ago. Patron and I would scrape up some money, get some OG Kush or some Sour Diesel, then have some crackhead give us his ride for a few hours for a few rocks and we'd drive to the beach. As I thought of this, I looked at my Gucci watch.

Out on the beach a beautiful woman was strolling. She looked like an actress, Jennifer Lawrence or Kendall Jenner. I felt I knew this woman, but her hair was darker. I walked out to my patio and down the steps, ignoring the fact that I had on four-hundred-dollar shoes and would be walking in the sand.

"Excuse me. Do I know you? I don't mean to be rude, but you're beautiful," I said amazed. I had not talked to a female since the issue with Shavonda. When she turned around, and I saw those gray eyes, then I knew. "Victoria?"

She was in an Alexander McQueen, one-piece purple bikini, with a purple shawl. A pair of Alexander McQueen slip-on shoes tied together, swung in her hand.

"Well, hello there, baby daddy," she said in her British accent. It was a sunny day and she looked gorgeous in the sunlight.

"What are you doing out here? I mean, I haven't seen you in quite some time," I said.

"What am I doing here? Well, it's a public beach, yuh know. I should have brought something to drink. I'm parched," she said, licking her sexy lips.

"Well, my condo is right over there. If you like, I could fix you a glass of lemonade," I said, showing every gold tooth I had.

"For your sake, I hope there is a splash of vodka in it. Girls love vodka," she said, sashaying past me.

Once in the condo, we chatted about things we had been up to. She had a modeling agency, and she was managing a few girls. I had opened up a bar not far from the beach. I still had the apartment duplex, E-City Towers and had a rap duo I was thinking of managing. When Paul never showed up, Milk Marie became the GM there. I didn't talk to her much, but I saw little Malcolm every weekend. We had half a bottle of Grey Goose, of course with the lemonade. I tried to take my eyes off her, but I couldn't. I checked my watch again, and she gave me a sad look.

"If I am disturbing something, my dear, I can make an exit. Even though," she said, undressing me with those gray eyes, "I love the company."

"Not at all. Just expecting a call," I said.

"Oh, well, in that case I have a question."

"Okay. Ask away," I said, sipping my Goose.

"Why haven't you kissed me yet?" she said with a frown.

"How do you know I want to kiss you?" I said, feeling the Goose.

"I'm a woman, my dear, and I would like very much to kiss you." Then she walked over to me. We kissed, then tore at each other's clothes. She devoured my manhood and refused to stop. Then she straddled me and shivered when she got on top. "Oh my God, mmm, yes, put it all in." She bucked on top of me. I could smell the perfume, Joy by Dior, which filled the room. That's what I felt. Joy. I can't lie. We fucked all over my condo, knocking things over. Once we both climaxed, she said, "I've never been with a black man, but it's definitely true what they say," she said giggling.

"And what do they say?" I said, laying on the living room floor grinning.

"Stop smiling," she said, hitting me. "All I know is I thought you were in my damn lungs, but I loved every minute of it. Listen, I know you have been through a lot, but I like you."

"Oh, after knocking over my furniture and draining me of my energy, you like me? Well, I wonder if you fell in love," I said, firing up some Purple. She looked at me for a long while.

"Shit, how do you know I can't? Hell, I've been hurt and cast away to the side. But I see the same hurt in your eyes. I'm a freak, true, but I am a grown ass woman and I'm here for you," she said, pulling my face so we were facing one another. For some reason, I believed her, but I was on point as well.

"So, what's the message? I mean, I am so glad you're the one delivering it," I said, watching her slip back in her Alexander McQueen.

She smiled at me. "And why do you think I have a message?" she asked, taking the blunt from me.

"Well, I'm on the outskirts of Virginia. Southern Shores Beach. I just happened to see you walk by, and I don't believe too much in coincidence," I said, slipping my pants on, tucking my Desert Eagle back in my waistline.

"Okay, okay," she said, looking at me with those gray eyes. "Wang says the hit on you is off from the Triad. They want to have a sit-down. I'm impressed, honestly." She passed the blunt back to me as I was putting my locks back in a ponytail.

"Impressed? And why is that?" I asked curiously.

"Because Fu Quan is head of the Triad, and you seem to have his attention. The hit on you has been off for quite some time though, you went off the grid. I did volunteer to come tell you."

"And the both of us screwing each other's brains out?" I said. She only laughed and looked me up and down.

"Of course, I had every intention of seducing you. I must say I'm thankful I came," she said slyly.

"To come sexually or come see me?" This is how it started. We flirted with words. I liked her.

"Why, my dear Yay. Of course," she said giggling. Her laugh was wonderful. "I want no lies between us, so you want to ask anything?"

"What's your connection with Han Che? And why would Wang send you?" Then it hit me. "You're Cartel?" She only nodded. Then she took a deep breath and began to speak.

"Years ago, I was singing in L.A., and I even was a model. A few commercials and modeling clothes. I met a Chinese guy, and he swept me off my feet. Time went by. He put his hand on me, but I was young and dumb. I thought I was in love." She wiped her eyes a bit. "Anyway, this man was of a different nationality. You see, because of the old ways, they wouldn't marry outside their race. But this man was also chasing another women. When I found out I was pregnant at only fifteen years old, my parents gave me a hard time, but I kept my babies."

"Babies, as in more than one?"

"Why, yes. I have twin boys. William and Lil Dave," she said. Then it hit me.

"You're Ying and Yang's mom? But you're gorgeous. I mean, you don't look like a mom," I said flabbergasted. She didn't look a day past twenty-five years old.

"Well, I am thirty now. I'll be thirty-one in two months. I was different then. As far as Ying and Yang, I never call them that. You see, He is their father," she said it, taking her eyes off mine.

"Holy shit! You're He's baby momma, the fucking guy who killed Charlotte, Han Che's wife?" I walked into the kitchen, opened up another bottle of Grey Goose. My head was spinning.

"Please let me explain. He killed Han Che's wife because he wanted her. He cut out her heart and sent it to Han Che. Because He could never leave the one thing."

"And that was her heart," I said, leaning on the fridge.

"Correct. My sons were treated like bastards and Han Che took us in. My boys proved their loyalty to the Cartel, and so did I," she said, eyes blazing with the memory of long-ago awakened anger.

"Jesus, you mean to tell me the twins killed their own father? So, that was the hit that put them in the Cartel? And that's why they have been assassins since kids?"

"True, but they delivered He to Han Che, and Han Che's men killed him. Since he took a souvenir, so did Han Che. This is why Fu Quan wants to speak to you. For a split second, they believed Han Che's spirit entered your body at the Museum. Obviously because of what you did," she said, taking the bottle from my hand. She got a glass and poured some of the clear liquid in it, then handed it to me.

"So, when do I have to meet the Triad?" I asked.

"There is a huge stadium a few miles from here. You have," she grabbed my wrist and looked at my Gucci watch, "two hours before you have to be there. It's only a thirty-minute drive." She looked at me seductively. "We have time to do this," she said, pulling her Alexander McQueen bikini down, exposing her voluptuous ass then bending over the counter. I put the glass down on the counter, and put it on her like a true G. I put my phone on the counter as well as expecting a call, while Victoria called out my name.

***

In the north side of Mojick, there was an old place where they kept fish and sharks, etc. It used to be a main attraction. It was called The Water Park. People could walk in and see dolphins, stingrays, etc. There was a walkway, and the see-through glass held the different kind of sea animals. But today was a different day.

"Why did you guys drag me out to this beat-up old water park? I hope you two are not planning to invest in this spot," Patron said, walking with Gucci Swagg and P-Funk.

"Hey, I might. You know it's a lot of money when people want to watch wildlife. You know white people love that shit," Gucci Swagg said laughing.

"Yes, and these rooms are airtight. Shit, even if you screamed, no one could hear you," P-Funk said, pulling out a .357, aiming at Patron.

"What the fuck you doing? Yo, when Yay find out you two trying to rob me, there will be hell to pay," Patron said, while Gucci Swagg disarmed him.

"Shut the fuck up and walk in that room," Gucci Swagg said, pointing Patron's own gun at him. "I'm already behind schedule." Gucci Swagg shoved Patron in the room, then locked the door. They looked at Patron through the glass, who was furious and beating on the glass. "You know who I am and how I get down. I told Yay not to fuck with car thieves."

He looked on the floor by a drain and saw a cell phone. There was a note on the phone. "Touch the screen to show video." Patron did what the message said, and the video began to play.

"If you are listening to this, you know now we are no longer brothers. You betrayed me in the worst way. Let me show you." Then a video of Shavonda and Patron having dinner at an expensive restaurant showed on the screen, and one of them kissing right when she was leaving. This was when Larry must have grabbed her. This was why she had the silver Iris Van Herpen dress on. The piece of shit even ratted to Shavonda about me and Milk Marie fucking. It explained Shavonda's attitude the next day. Then the video went off.

"You piece of shit. You put Dickerson on Ken Chew, looking to cut a deal after I got extorted, but Dickerson thought we were hot. You kept telling me to go to Atlanta, because if I went down with Ken Chew, then you could run off with Shavonda. Tell Dickerson I said hello." The floor started filling with water. It was cold and now up to Patron's knees and getting higher. Something bit him, then again. There were piranhas in the aquarium vault Patron was locked in. Patron tried to scream and yell, but the water was now over his head.

Gucci Swagg and P-Funk were smoking a blunt watching. P-Funk was recording it while making a bet with Gucci Swagg.

"I bet you he lasts three more minutes," P-Funk said.

"Hundred bucks say he done in another minute. Shit, he already jerking and shaking." As the piranhas were feasting on Patron's flesh, one went in his mouth and chewed its way out his neck.

"Fuck," P-Funk said, giving up the hundred-dollar-bill.

"Easy money, playboy. Now call Yay and let him know it's done," Gucci Swagg said, looking at what was left of Patron. Blood filled the aquarium. "Patron," Gucci Swagg said, "you now swim with the fishes," in Tony Montana's *Scarface* voice.

"Yo, you called Yay? I'm saving this video, then I'll send it to his phone," P-Funk said, still tapping the phone as they both got in the Porsche truck. As they drove off, Gucci Swagg called Yay up.

***

I had just finished breaking Victoria off for the second time, when my phone rang.

"Yo, what up, playboy? What's good? P-Funk 'bout to send you a video," Gucci Swagg said, talking to me on FaceTime. I picked up my other phone, looked at the video, and then deleted it.

"Okay, cool. Now I am on my way to a meeting with the Triad, and all the shit that popped off in Atlanta will be a memory," I said, popping Victoria on the ass as she walked by.

"Yo, um, is that the British chic? Bruh, is that the bitch that look like Emma Stone?" Gucci Swagg said, eyeballing Victoria walking by with that plump ass.

"Yo, Gucci Swagg, cut the shenanigans, homie. She foreign. She British, not a bitch," I said, trying not to laugh because Gucci Swagg was my dude.

"Nigguh, is that the bitch that look like Emma Stone? The chic with the English accent?" Gucci Swagg and now P-Funk were on the screen. I glanced at Victoria and yes, she was beautiful.

"Yes, man, more like a young Sharon Stone. Look, I got to go. You fools get off my phone," I said laughing.

"Okay. Okay, Yay, but I got one thing to say," Gucci Swagg said.

"What, man?" I said, getting ready to leave.

"Abruh kuh dabruh!" Then Gucci Swagg and P-Funk hung up. I was still laughing because *Half Baked* was one of my favorite movies. When David Chapelle kept saying, "Abruh kuh dabruh," shit had me weak.

"Friends of yours, my sweet? The boys having a giggle since you got my goodies?" Victoria said seductively. It was so sexy the way she sarcastically described things.

"I think my homies approve of all your… um," then my eyes roamed up and down her figure, "assets, I believe."

I changed clothes to an all-black Gucci suit with both Desert Eagles on my hip. I felt my outfit was complete. Victoria had gone to her Jaguar, where she always kept a change of clothes. She was in a maroon dress, which was my favorite color. It was a velvet jacquard strapless dress, costing three grand. I put my hair in a ponytail, still glowing off the shower we took together.

"Why are you looking at me that way?" Victoria said.

"Shit, with what that dress cost, I'm wondering if I can afford you," I said, joking while walking to the deep freezer, putting my package in a Gucci book sack.

"Oh, trust me, baby," she said, patting my behind. "You can afford me. Lucky for you, I have my own money. What's in the book sack?" Victoria said as we left the condo. I opened the door to my gray Hummer for her to get in.

"Oh, just a housewarming gift for our meeting."

Once we were at this stadium, all kinds of cars were parked outside. Mostly Benz, Lexus, Jeeps, Tahoes, and a few BMWs. Of course, I knew who the Maybach belonged to. As we walked in, four Chinese gentlemen were at the door. They patted us down, thankfully not taking my guns.

Seems Victoria had a .380 taped to her thigh, but we were guests, and it was weird they never asked what was in the bag. There was this huge round table and on one end, Wang sat with Fujj, as well as fifteen of his own men. There were candles burning all through the room. I took my backpack off and sat down. Victoria sat down beside me, being there were only two seats available. The four Chinese men stayed at the door, then a very slim man with a very long beard stood up. He was handsome, like a Chinese Ice-T. Everyone went quiet when he stood. Then I knew I was in a room with the most dangerous men on the planet. The room was filled with killers.

Wang and Fujj nodded at me as I nodded back. I noticed the twins a few seats from Wang. If they disapproved with me showing up with their mother, they didn't show it. Everyone had their game faces on, then Fu Quan spoke.

"We have feuded long enough, and the Triad plans to call a truce. May old things begin new after this day. Mr. Yayo Sun, we finally have the pleasure to meet. I didn't like two of my own dying in some museum." Then Fu Quan glanced at Wang. "But I received the DNA. I know all about Han and his evil intentions. He was planning to start a war."

Fu Quan walked toward me and the four Chinese at the door started to move, but Fu Quan waved at them to stand their post. Once Fu Quan was in front of me, he rubbed his beard like the guy that trained Uma Thurman in the movie *Kill Bill*.

"Yayo Sun, there is a story called 'The Sword of the Samurai.' Contrary to what many think, the essence of leadership lies in serving. Leaders must work harder than others. You,

Yayo Sun, are a leader with boldness and value, performance over pedigree. The secret to dedication is give everything to the task. For that, we all salute you." At that moment, everyone stood up and bowed.

"The Cartel and Triad are now at peace," Fu Quan said, going back to his seat but still standing. "If you have any words, you may speak."

All eyes were on me, and I wasn't about long speeches. So many had died and so many had gone through hell. I looked at Wang and Fujj, who seemed to be waiting for me to speak. I picked up the Gucci sack and opened it. I ripped the plastic off and I said, "To betray one another will not be tolerated. The penalty is death." Then I pulled Han's, aka Ken Chew's head out of the backpack. I sat it on the table, and I bowed as Fu Quan did to me. "Long live Han Che."

***

A Few Months Later...

I made sure Lisa was financially good. Patron's sins were not her sins. I'd paid for Shavonda's funeral, but I had no idea where she was buried. Honestly, it didn't bother me. I had buried good and bad. Victoria and I were in Porto Ercole, Italy. Rumor was the famous actor, Cary Grant, came out there to tan after filming.

There was this Mediterranean cliff elevator. The whole damn cliff moved, and I was impressed. We also had plans to go to Athens. Victoria was swimming. Ying came up to me.

"Look, if you want, you can call me William. I think it's cool, you and my mom chilling," he said as I passed the blunt of Moonrock. Yang came up beside us, his dark hair down his back. We were all shirtless with shorts on.

Yang added, "Well, just because you banging my mom, I'm not going to call you Dad or no shit like that." We all started laughing. The day was beautiful, and I was thankful to enjoy it.

"Well, can I join in on the laugh?" Victoria said with a Louis Vuitton bathing suit on, hair spilling in waves down her back.

Ying had his mother's hair. Yang had He's hair.

"Just talking men talk with the boys," I said, watching Ying pass the blunt to Yang. There were four glasses and Grey Goose on ice. Victoria poured Grey Goose in all our glasses and said, "A toast to my sweets."

We all lifted our glasses. "To new beginnings," then we all took a drink.

"And to the Cartel," Yang said. We all clinked our glasses again and drank.

I then took a walk on the beach. So much betrayal, so many lies. When would it end? Then I heard Ying come up behind me.

"What's up, Ying?" I said.

"Only you can call me William," Ying said.

"Okay then, William. What's up?"

"I know a lot of people betrayed you, used you, and lied to you. But my mom, my brother, and I will never turn our backs on you or betray you," Ying said.

"I believe you, and I will hold you to that," I said as he hugged me.

Yang came up to us. "What's all the mushy stuff, man? Mom wants to sightsee some more," Yang said and his voice changed. "Yay, I have never seen my mom this happy. I just want to say thank you."

"No problem." I gave him and Ying some dap.

"Broke niggas make noise," I said.

"But rich niggas make moves!" the twins said at the same time.

To Be Continued...
Betrayal of a Thug 3
Coming Soon

About the Author

FRE$H, Samuel Geddie, is from the rough streets of Webbtown—Goldsboro, NC, U.S.A. FRE$H is also the author of several other novels, including:

Betrayal of a Thug Vol. I

Betrayal of a Thug Vol. II: The Search for Han

Do What I Got To Do.

Expect more soon and view his writing on Amazon.

Lock Down Publications and Ca$h Presents assisted
publishing packages.

BASIC PACKAGE $499

Editing

Cover Design

Formatting

UPGRADED PACKAGE $800

Typing

Editing

Cover Design

Formatting

ADVANCE PACKAGE $1,200

Typing

Editing

Cover Design

Formatting

Copyright registration

Proofreading

Betrayal of a Thug 2

Upload book to Amazon

LDP SUPREME PACKAGE $1,500

Typing

Editing

Cover Design

Formatting

Copyright registration

Proofreading

Set up Amazon account

Upload book to Amazon

Advertise on LDP Amazon and Facebook page

***Other services available upon request. Additional charges may apply

Lock Down Publications

P.O. Box 944

Stockbridge, GA 30281-9998

Phone # 470 303-9761

Submission Guideline

Submit the first three chapters of your completed manuscript to ldpsubmissions@gmail.com, subject line: Your book's title. The manuscript must be in a .doc file and sent as an attachment. Document should be in Times New Roman, double spaced and in size 12 font. Also, provide your synopsis and full contact information. If sending multiple submissions, they must each be in a separate email.

Have a story but no way to send it electronically? You can still submit to LDP/Ca$h Presents. Send in the first three chapters, written or typed, of your completed manuscript to:

LDP: Submissions Dept
Po Box 944
Stockbridge, Ga 30281

DO NOT send original manuscript. Must be a duplicate.

Provide your synopsis and a cover letter containing your full contact information.

Thanks for considering LDP and Ca$h Presents.

<u>NEW RELEASES</u>

BABY, I'M WINTERTIME COLD by MEESHA

ANGEL 4 by ANTHONY FIELDS

HOOD CONSIGLIERE 2 by KEESE

KILLA KOUNTY by KHUFU

BETRAYAL OF A THUG 2 by FRE$H

Fre$h

166

Betrayal of a Thug 2

By **T.J. Edwards**
GORILLAZ IN THE BAY V
3X KRAZY III
STRAIGHT BEAST MODE III
De'Kari
KINGPIN KILLAZ IV
STREET KINGS III
PAID IN BLOOD III
CARTEL KILLAZ IV
DOPE GODS III
Hood Rich
SINS OF A HUSTLA II
ASAD
RICH $AVAGE III
By Martell Troublesome Bolden
YAYO V
Bred In The Game 2
S. Allen
THE STREETS WILL TALK II
By Yolanda Moore
SON OF A DOPE FIEND III
HEAVEN GOT A GHETTO II
SKI MASK MONEY II
By Renta
LOYALTY AIN'T PROMISED III
By Keith Williams
I'M NOTHING WITHOUT HIS LOVE II

SINS OF A THUG II

TO THE THUG I LOVED BEFORE II

IN A HUSTLER I TRUST II

By Monet Dragun

QUIET MONEY IV

EXTENDED CLIP III

THUG LIFE IV

By **Trai'Quan**

THE STREETS MADE ME IV

By **Larry D. Wright**

IF YOU CROSS ME ONCE II

ANGEL V

By **Anthony Fields**

THE STREETS WILL NEVER CLOSE IV

By K'ajji

HARD AND RUTHLESS III

KILLA KOUNTY IV

By Khufu

MONEY GAME III

By Smoove Dolla

JACK BOYS VS DOPE BOYS IV

A GANGSTA'S QUR'AN V

COKE GIRLZ II

COKE BOYS II

LIFE OF A SAVAGE V

CHI'RAQ GANGSTAS V

By Romell Tukes

MURDA WAS THE CASE III

Elijah R. Freeman

THE STREETS NEVER LET GO III

By Robert Baptiste

AN UNFORESEEN LOVE IV

BABY, I'M WINTERTIME COLD II

By **Meesha**

MONEY MAFIA II

By **Jibril Williams**

QUEEN OF THE ZOO III

By **Black Migo**

VICIOUS LOYALTY III

By Kingpen

A GANGSTA'S PAIN III

By J-Blunt

CONFESSIONS OF A JACKBOY III

By Nicholas Lock

GRIMEY WAYS III

By Ray Vinci

KING KILLA II

By Vincent "Vitto" Holloway

BETRAYAL OF A THUG III

By Fre$h

THE MURDER QUEENS III

By Michael Gallon

THE BIRTH OF A GANGSTER III

By Delmont Player

TREAL LOVE II

By Le'Monica Jackson

FOR THE LOVE OF BLOOD II

By Jamel Mitchell

RAN OFF ON DA PLUG II

By Paper Boi Rari

HOOD CONSIGLIERE III

By Keese

PRETTY GIRLS DO NASTY THINGS II

By Nicole Goosby

PROTÉGÉ OF A LEGEND II

By Corey Robinson

IT'S JUST ME AND YOU II

By Ah'Million

BORN IN THE GRAVE II

By Self Made Tay

FOREVER GANGSTA III

By Adrian Dulan

GORILLAZ IN THE TRENCHES II

By SayNoMore

Available Now

RESTRAINING ORDER **I & II**

By **CA$H & Coffee**

LOVE KNOWS NO BOUNDARIES **I II & III**

By **Coffee**

RAISED AS A GOON I, II, III & IV

BRED BY THE SLUMS I, II, III

BLAST FOR ME I & II

ROTTEN TO THE CORE I II III

A BRONX TALE I, II, III

DUFFLE BAG CARTEL I II III IV V VI

HEARTLESS GOON I II III IV V

A SAVAGE DOPEBOY I II

DRUG LORDS I II III

CUTTHROAT MAFIA I II

KING OF THE TRENCHES

By **Ghost**

LAY IT DOWN **I & II**

LAST OF A DYING BREED I II

BLOOD STAINS OF A SHOTTA I & II III

By **Jamaica**

LOYAL TO THE GAME I II III

LIFE OF SIN I, II III

By **TJ & Jelissa**

BLOODY COMMAS I & II

SKI MASK CARTEL I II & III

KING OF NEW YORK I II,III IV V

RISE TO POWER I II III

COKE KINGS I II III IV V

BORN HEARTLESS I II III IV

KING OF THE TRAP I II

By **T.J. Edwards**

IF LOVING HIM IS WRONG…I & II

LOVE ME EVEN WHEN IT HURTS I II III

By **Jelissa**

WHEN THE STREETS CLAP BACK I & II III

THE HEART OF A SAVAGE I II III IV

MONEY MAFIA

LOYAL TO THE SOIL I II III

By **Jibril Williams**

A DISTINGUISHED THUG STOLE MY HEART I II & III

LOVE SHOULDN'T HURT I II III IV

RENEGADE BOYS I II III IV

PAID IN KARMA I II III

SAVAGE STORMS I II III

AN UNFORESEEN LOVE I II III

BABY, I'M WINTERTIME COLD

By **Meesha**

A GANGSTER'S CODE I &, II III

A GANGSTER'S SYN I II III

THE SAVAGE LIFE I II III

CHAINED TO THE STREETS I II III

Betrayal of a Thug 2

BLOOD ON THE MONEY I II III

A GANGSTA'S PAIN I II

By J-Blunt

PUSH IT TO THE LIMIT

By **Bre' Hayes**

BLOOD OF A BOSS **I, II, III, IV, V**

SHADOWS OF THE GAME

TRAP BASTARD

By **Askari**

THE STREETS BLEED MURDER **I, II & III**

THE HEART OF A GANGSTA I II& III

By **Jerry Jackson**

CUM FOR ME I II III IV V VI VII VIII

An **LDP Erotica Collaboration**

BRIDE OF A HUSTLA **I II & II**

THE FETTI GIRLS **I, II& III**

CORRUPTED BY A GANGSTA I, II III, IV

BLINDED BY HIS LOVE

THE PRICE YOU PAY FOR LOVE I, II ,III

DOPE GIRL MAGIC I II III

By **Destiny Skai**

WHEN A GOOD GIRL GOES BAD

By **Adrienne**

THE COST OF LOYALTY I II III

By Kweli

A GANGSTER'S REVENGE **I II III & IV**

THE BOSS MAN'S DAUGHTERS I II III IV V

Fre$h

A SAVAGE LOVE **I & II**

BAE BELONGS TO ME I II

A HUSTLER'S DECEIT I, II, III

WHAT BAD BITCHES DO I, II, III

SOUL OF A MONSTER I II III

KILL ZONE

A DOPE BOY'S QUEEN I II III

TIL DEATH

By **Aryanna**

A KINGPIN'S AMBITON

A KINGPIN'S AMBITION **II**

I MURDER FOR THE DOUGH

By **Ambitious**

TRUE SAVAGE I II III IV V VI VII

DOPE BOY MAGIC I, II, III

MIDNIGHT CARTEL I II III

CITY OF KINGZ I II

NIGHTMARE ON SILENT AVE

THE PLUG OF LIL MEXICO II

CLASSIC CITY

By **Chris Green**

A DOPEBOY'S PRAYER

By **Eddie "Wolf" Lee**

THE KING CARTEL **I, II & III**

By **Frank Gresham**

THESE NIGGAS AIN'T LOYAL **I, II & III**

By **Nikki Tee**

GANGSTA SHYT **I II &III**

By **CATO**

THE ULTIMATE BETRAYAL

By **Phoenix**

BOSS'N UP **I , II & III**

By **Royal Nicole**

I LOVE YOU TO DEATH

By **Destiny J**

I RIDE FOR MY HITTA

I STILL RIDE FOR MY HITTA

By **Misty Holt**

LOVE & CHASIN' PAPER

By **Qay Crockett**

TO DIE IN VAIN

SINS OF A HUSTLA

By **ASAD**

BROOKLYN HUSTLAZ

By **Boogsy Morina**

BROOKLYN ON LOCK I & II

By **Sonovia**

GANGSTA CITY

By **Teddy Duke**

A DRUG KING AND HIS DIAMOND I & II III

A DOPEMAN'S RICHES

HER MAN, MINE'S TOO I, II

CASH MONEY HO'S

THE WIFEY I USED TO BE I II

PRETTY GIRLS DO NASTY THINGS

By Nicole Goosby

TRAPHOUSE KING **I II & III**

KINGPIN KILLAZ I II III

STREET KINGS I II

PAID IN BLOOD **I II**

CARTEL KILLAZ I II III

DOPE GODS I II

By **Hood Rich**

LIPSTICK KILLAH **I, II, III**

CRIME OF PASSION I II & III

FRIEND OR FOE I II III

By **Mimi**

STEADY MOBBN' **I, II, III**

THE STREETS STAINED MY SOUL I II III

By **Marcellus Allen**

WHO SHOT YA **I, II, III**

SON OF A DOPE FIEND I II

HEAVEN GOT A GHETTO

SKI MASK MONEY

Renta

GORILLAZ IN THE BAY **I II III IV**

TEARS OF A GANGSTA I II

3X KRAZY I II

STRAIGHT BEAST MODE I II

DE'KARI

TRIGGADALE I II III

Betrayal of a Thug 2

MURDAROBER WAS THE CASE I II
Elijah R. Freeman
GOD BLESS THE TRAPPERS I, II, III
THESE SCANDALOUS STREETS I, II, III
FEAR MY GANGSTA I, II, III IV, V
THESE STREETS DON'T LOVE NOBODY I, II
BURY ME A G I, II, III, IV, V
A GANGSTA'S EMPIRE I, II, III, IV
THE DOPEMAN'S BODYGAURD I II
THE REALEST KILLAZ I II III
THE LAST OF THE OGS I II III
Tranay Adams
THE STREETS ARE CALLING
Duquie Wilson
MARRIED TO A BOSS I II III
By Destiny Skai & Chris Green
KINGZ OF THE GAME I II III IV V VI
Playa Ray
SLAUGHTER GANG I II III
RUTHLESS HEART I II III
By Willie Slaughter
FUK SHYT
By Blakk Diamond
DON'T F#CK WITH MY HEART I II
By Linnea
ADDICTED TO THE DRAMA I II III
IN THE ARM OF HIS BOSS II

Fre$h

By Jamila

YAYO I II III IV

A SHOOTER'S AMBITION I II

BRED IN THE GAME

By S. Allen

TRAP GOD I II III

RICH $AVAGE I II

MONEY IN THE GRAVE I II III

By Martell Troublesome Bolden

FOREVER GANGSTA I II

GLOCKS ON SATIN SHEETS I II

By Adrian Dulan

TOE TAGZ I II III IV

LEVELS TO THIS SHYT I II

IT'S JUST ME AND YOU

By Ah'Million

KINGPIN DREAMS I II III

RAN OFF ON DA PLUG

By Paper Boi Rari

CONFESSIONS OF A GANGSTA I II III IV

CONFESSIONS OF A JACKBOY I II

By Nicholas Lock

I'M NOTHING WITHOUT HIS LOVE

SINS OF A THUG

TO THE THUG I LOVED BEFORE

A GANGSTA SAVED XMAS

IN A HUSTLER I TRUST

Betrayal of a Thug 2

By Monet Dragun

CAUGHT UP IN THE LIFE I II III

THE STREETS NEVER LET GO I II

By Robert Baptiste

NEW TO THE GAME I II III

MONEY, MURDER & MEMORIES I II III

By Malik D. Rice

LIFE OF A SAVAGE I II III IV

A GANGSTA'S QUR'AN I II III IV

MURDA SEASON I II III

GANGLAND CARTEL I II III

CHI'RAQ GANGSTAS I II III IV

KILLERS ON ELM STREET I II III

JACK BOYZ N DA BRONX I II III

A DOPEBOY'S DREAM I II III

JACK BOYS VS DOPE BOYS I II III

COKE GIRLZ

COKE BOYS

By Romell Tukes

LOYALTY AIN'T PROMISED I II

By Keith Williams

QUIET MONEY I II III

THUG LIFE I II III

EXTENDED CLIP I II

A GANGSTA'S PARADISE

By Trai'Quan

THE STREETS MADE ME I II III

By **Larry D. Wright**
THE ULTIMATE SACRIFICE I, II, III, IV, V, VI
KHADIFI
IF YOU CROSS ME ONCE
ANGEL I II III IV
IN THE BLINK OF AN EYE
By **Anthony Fields**
THE LIFE OF A HOOD STAR
By **Ca$h & Rashia Wilson**
THE STREETS WILL NEVER CLOSE I II III
By **K'ajji**
CREAM I II III
THE STREETS WILL TALK
By **Yolanda Moore**
NIGHTMARES OF A HUSTLA I II III
By **King Dream**
CONCRETE KILLA I II III
VICIOUS LOYALTY I II
By **Kingpen**
HARD AND RUTHLESS I II
MOB TOWN 251
THE BILLIONAIRE BENTLEYS I II III
By **Von Diesel**
GHOST MOB
Stilloan Robinson
MOB TIES I II III IV V VI
SOUL OF A HUSTLER, HEART OF A KILLER

GORILLAZ IN THE TRENCHES
By SayNoMore
BODYMORE MURDERLAND I II III
THE BIRTH OF A GANGSTER I II
By Delmont Player
FOR THE LOVE OF A BOSS
By C. D. Blue
MOBBED UP I II III IV
THE BRICK MAN I II III IV
THE COCAINE PRINCESS I II III IV V
By King Rio
KILLA KOUNTY I II III IV
By Khufu
MONEY GAME I II
By Smoove Dolla
A GANGSTA'S KARMA I II
By FLAME
KING OF THE TRENCHES I II III
by **GHOST & TRANAY ADAMS**
QUEEN OF THE ZOO I II
By **Black Migo**
GRIMEY WAYS I II
By Ray Vinci
XMAS WITH AN ATL SHOOTER
By Ca$h & Destiny Skai
KING KILLA
By Vincent "Vitto" Holloway

Fre$h

BETRAYAL OF A THUG I II
By Fre$h
THE MURDER QUEENS I II
By Michael Gallon
TREAL LOVE
By Le'Monica Jackson
FOR THE LOVE OF BLOOD
By Jamel Mitchell
HOOD CONSIGLIERE I II
By Keese
PROTÉGÉ OF A LEGEND
By Corey Robinson
BORN IN THE GRAVE
By Self Made Tay
MOAN IN MY MOUTH
By XTASY
TORN BETWEEN A GANGSTER AND A GENTLEMAN
By J-BLUNT & Miss Kim

<u>BOOKS BY LDP'S CEO, CA$H</u>

TRUST IN NO MAN

TRUST IN NO MAN 2

TRUST IN NO MAN 3

BONDED BY BLOOD

SHORTY GOT A THUG

THUGS CRY

THUGS CRY 2

THUGS CRY 3

TRUST NO BITCH

TRUST NO BITCH 2

TRUST NO BITCH 3

TIL MY CASKET DROPS

RESTRAINING ORDER

RESTRAINING ORDER 2

IN LOVE WITH A CONVICT

LIFE OF A HOOD STAR

XMAS WITH AN ATL SHOOTER

Fre$h

www.ingramcontent.com/pod-product-compliance
Lightning Source LLC
Chambersburg PA
CBHW070520260626
47161CB00004B/1602